"Why...

"This is hardly the time for discussion, Julie," Colin answered, pushing her toward the incline and the copse of trees.

"But I don't understand—"

"What's to understand? Run, *now*!"

She could hear the engine behind her, roaring louder, the lights growing brighter as the car approached. In the distance, sirens shrieked. George, the night watchman, must have noticed the ruckus and called the police. But there was no time to wait for them now. Julie stepped forward, landing in a hole and nearly collapsing to the ground. "Oh!" Pain shot through her ankle like fire.

"What's the matter?" Colin asked.

"I've twisted my ankle."

"Darn!" He glanced back. The car careered down the embankment just a few yards from them. The glare of the headlights had become a glimmer of death.

"He's going to kill us," Julie said.

"Not if I can help it," Colin swore.

ABOUT THE AUTHOR

Although Jan Michaels is from Kentucky, she considers herself a transplanted Yankee and has called Chicago her home for most of her life. In addition to being an author, Jan is a wife, mother, volunteer, registered nurse and unregistered chauffeur—not necessarily in that order. She has been published under the pseudonym Jan Mathews and believes there's no finer mix than cops-and-robbers and romance. The author enjoys hearing from readers, and letters will be forwarded to her if they are sent to Harlequin's New York office. *Into the Night* is Jan's fourth Intrigue novel.

Books by Jan Michaels

HARLEQUIN INTRIGUE
32–PURSUIT IN THE WILDERNESS
71–THE ONLY WITNESS
89–RED DOG RUN

Don't miss any of our special offers. Write to us at the following address for information on our newest releases.

Harlequin Reader Service
901 Fuhrmann Blvd., P.O. Box 1397, Buffalo, NY 14240
Canadian address: P.O. Box 603,
Fort Erie, Ont. L2A 5X3

Into the Night
Jan Michaels

Harlequin Books

TORONTO • NEW YORK • LONDON
AMSTERDAM • PARIS • SYDNEY • HAMBURG
STOCKHOLM • ATHENS • TOKYO • MILAN

For all those friends who have supported my career, this one's for you: my cousin Debbie, Karen's Debbie, Norvette, Lynn and Judy, Lynn and Linda, Theo and Ruth, Mary Kay Prette, Sandy Brand, Geri Hansen and Ann Reutenauer, Vera and Bill and all the people at Dooley, my Aunt Mary Lu, my Aunt Ruth, my cousin, Ginny, Maureen, Rose and Cathy from writer's group, and lastly, Julie, for whom the heroine is named. Thank you all!

Harlequin Intrigue edition published August 1988

ISBN 0-373-22096-0

Copyright © 1988 Jan Milella. All rights reserved. Except for use in any review, the reproduction or utilization of this work in whole or in part in any form by any electronic, mechanical or other means, now known or hereafter invented, including xerography, photocopying and recording, or in any information storage or retrieval system, is forbidden without the permission of the publisher, Harlequin Enterprises Limited, 225 Duncan Mill Road, Don Mills, Ontario, Canada M3B 3K9, or Harlequin Books, P.O. Box 958, North Sydney, Australia 2060.

All the characters in this book have no existence outside the imagination of the author and have no relation whatsoever to anyone bearing the same name or names. They are not even distantly inspired by any individual known or unknown to the author, and all incidents are pure invention.

® are Trademarks registered in the United States Patent and Trademark Office and in other countries.

Printed in U.S.A.

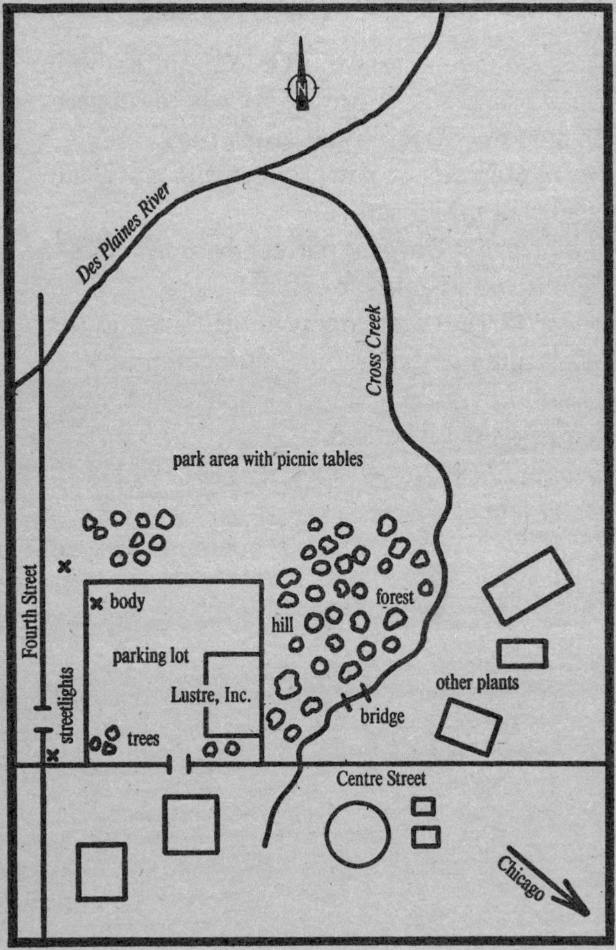

Des Plaines River
N
Cross Creek
park area with picnic tables
Fourth Street
body
forest
hill
parking lot
Lustre, Inc.
streetlights
trees
other plants
bridge
Centre Street
Chicago

CAST OF CHARACTERS

Julie Hunter—She strolled into a murder setup.

Colin Marshall—A private eye who'd rubbed one too many crooks the wrong way.

Norm Osgood—A pawnbroker with a private chauffeur *after* death.

Brad Davis—Devoted partner *extraordinaire* or fiendish mind going for glory?

Roger Perry—Vacationing in the Bahamas that bleak summer day, or committing murder?

Virgil Thompson—Bland foreman, his loyalty verged on the fanatical.

George Ellsworth—A security guard with a shaky aim.

Detective Meier—He wasn't about to chase an elusive corpse.

Chapter One

All her life Julie Hunter had been fortunate enough to have avoided funerals. She had never seen a corpse, but the man lying still and silent near the edge of the parking lot had to be dead. She knew it as surely as she was breathing. Just as she knew the man crouched over the body was his killer.

The night was dark and riddled with stormclouds. The rain seemed incessant. Lightning bolted in bright, angry streaks across the sky and thunder rolled loudly. She had left her office a few minutes ago, late, picking her way through the puddles and holding her briefcase over her head so her hair wouldn't get wet.

Every time a bit of precipitation hit, her long red hair would frizz up into kinky curls. In a few more minutes she would resemble a Kewpie doll. She shoved the heavy mass back from her face. She could see an object vaguely in the light of the streetlamp, and she paused beside her car. Something had made her stop and look, some eerie movement over near a copse of trees. A noise, nothing loud, perhaps a soft footfall, as though someone were sneaking up on her. Or sneaking away. But stormy nights tended to frighten her, as did dark shadowy parking lots.

Then she saw him, lying there, face up.

His eyes stared vacantly into space and his mouth was frozen open in an expression of agony, like that painting she'd seen in the Art Institute downtown. Blood drenched the front of his once-white shirt and spread out around him in a pool, mingling with the rain that had pelted Chicago the past couple of days. They formed a crimson river that swirled down a sewer drain a few yards away.

"Oh, my God," Julie murmured, paralyzed with fear. Thunder crashed again, covering the sound of her heels on the cement as she stepped backward.

The tall, blond-haired man who had knelt over the dead man didn't know she was there. Crimson splattered his coat and streaked his hands as he pressed the other man's throat, obviously feeling for a pulse. Quickly he searched the sprawled body, looking for something hidden in a coat or pants pocket.

Frightened by the grotesque sight, certain now that the man was dead, Julie dropped both her briefcase and keys, intending to run. The clatter could be heard over the rain, and the killer glanced up, staring straight at her. She couldn't help but notice his muscular build and attractive good looks. A thin, pale scar ran down his cheek, and his eyes bored into her, hard and penetrating. She shivered, then watched him rise to his full height. The gun clutched in his right hand was pointed straight at her.

"Oh, God," she murmured, swallowing hard.

At five feet seven inches, Julie was tall for a woman and in good shape. She had always prided herself on knowing when to take a stand and when to run. Now was a time to run. She started to back away. After all, the man was surely dead, while she was alive—which might not be for long if she stuck around.

Raindrops pelting her, water streaming down her face and hair, her heart pounding, she whirled and ran, sprinting as if all the demons of hell were dogging her footsteps.

"Help!" she screamed, heading back toward the building in the distance. Her high-heeled shoes splashed through the water, loudly now. "George, help!"

Normally the old man they had hired to keep an eye on the place at night sat at the front desk and talked on the phone. If only she could reach him.

"Damn!" she heard the blond-haired man swear.

Julie knew without looking that he had started after her. She could hear him behind, his heavy footsteps hitting the pavement. He lunged for her and just narrowly missed the edge of her coat. Goaded on, she ran faster, so fast her legs ached and her lungs were bursting. She arrived at the door to her building huffing and puffing, and banged against the glass.

"George!" she shouted a second time, rattling the doorknob and glancing behind her. Surprisingly the parking lot was empty. No one was there. Where had the man gone? He had wanted to kill her. He had chased her. Would he jump out any moment and strangle her? She had to get away. "Hurry, George!" She banged harder on the glass. "Help! Let me in!"

When the white-haired guard opened the door for her, she nearly fell into his arms with relief. "Oh!" she gasped. "Thank goodness you're here."

"What's the matter, Miss Hunter?" The elderly man frowned at her in concern. "Is something wrong?"

Julie could hardly speak. "There's—there's a dead man in the parking lot."

"A dead man?" The guard's frown deepened. "Goodness. Are you all right, Miss Hunter?"

She had started trembling, either from the cold or from fear, she wasn't certain which, and she was panting, trying to catch her breath. "Yes, yes, I'm fine," she answered, sucking in air. Her clothes were soaked, and because her raincoat had fallen open the sea-green silk charmeuse shirtwaist dress she wore was ruined. Her leather shoes were soaked through, never to be the same again. "But there's—there's a killer out there. And a dead man." She'd never been more frightened in her life.

The guard peered out the door into the dark, stormy night. "A killer? Here? Where at?"

"At the edge of the parking lot. I saw him. And I—I saw a... There was a man kneeling over a body. I—we—" Julie pushed back her sodden hair, trying to think, trying to breathe. She whirled around, realizing she wasn't at all safe. "Quick, lock the doors and get away from the window! He might get in. We have to call the police."

"But maybe I should—"

"No! Don't go out there." Scurrying around the elderly man, she closed and locked the door herself. "The killer's still out there. He's got a gun. I don't want you to get hurt."

She grabbed the phone and dialed the police. In a shrill voice she described what had happened. Assured they would arrive shortly, she hung up.

"Maybe we should hide," she went on, thinking of how vulnerable they were. "Quick. Get behind the desk."

Carrying the phone with her, she pushed George behind the heavy piece of furniture before he could object. "What are you doing?" he asked when she dialed another number.

"Calling Brad." Thank goodness one of her two partners at Lustre, Inc., a silver reclamation plant just outside Chicago, lived close by. He carried an emergency beeper to signal him to return to the plant—a necessity in case of cyanide accidents. She dialed the code and hung up.

It was only a matter of minutes before the police arrived—five minutes at the most. Not until later would Julie marvel at the surprising response time, highly unusual for the tiny suburban police force. The dispatcher had to have called out every squad car in the vicinity, for at least ten cars squealed into the parking lot and surrounded the building, lights blazing and sirens blaring. Even over the thunder and lightning Julie could hear their voices and footsteps as they approached, rifles cocked. People were running in all directions and shouting.

The next thing she knew someone burst through the front door. There were only two entrances to the plant, the back way, which required a special key, and the reception area, where Julie and the security guard had been hiding. Several offices, separated by doors, were located between the plant itself and the reception area. She ducked when a voice shouted, "Police! Anyone here?"

George waved from behind the desk. "We're here."

Julie inched out, and George followed suit, straightening his cramped long legs. Suddenly a short stocky man emerged from the back of the plant, running a hand through his thinning hair in confusion.

"Wait, don't shoot!" Julie cried, worried that the policeman, already jumpy, might be trigger-happy. "That's Virgil, the plant manager. He's okay."

Her instincts were right. The policeman relaxed visibly. By then more officers had arrived. She counted about a baker's dozen, clumped together like Keystone Cops, until one of them, probably the commander, stepped out and started issuing orders. They split into groups to search the plant and office area.

"Miss Hunter? George?" Virgil asked, stumbling up to Julie, who was leaning against the desk, fear in her face. "What's going on? What are they doing here?"

"There's a killer," George told him. "Quick, hide."

"No need." The policeman who'd been issuing orders holstered his gun as he approached Julie and the others. "It looks clear, though we'll know for certain in a moment."

Julie was distraught. "Please tell your men, Captain, to be careful. There are cyanide vats back there."

The dangerous chemical was used to recover silver from film. It sat in huge lead-lined containers, but there was always danger of a spill. The hose leading to the chemical could get knocked off the wall holder, spraying poison into the room, or a vat could tip over. Death would then occur in minutes. Even though precautions were taken, Julie was always afraid someone would get hurt. It was too easy to have an accident.

"They're aware of it," the policeman answered. "Are you all right, miss?"

"Fine." She felt foolish about the way she'd hidden behind the desk, so cowardlike. Yet in spite of the police she glanced toward the window cautiously. Lights blazed like broad daylight, illuminating the parking lot and throwing the building into relief. "What's going on?"

"Just securing the area," he told her. He wore a blue uniform, and his paunch made the buttons on his jacket look as if they were going to pop. "Nothing to be concerned about. We're searching for the suspect."

A few minutes later another policeman came in. This one was older, perhaps middle-aged. He wore street clothes with a yellow rain slicker overtop, and he carried an old umbrella. He shook it out and turned to her, holding out her briefcase and keys. "These belong to you, I believe?"

She nodded. "Yes, thank you."

"You're Julie Hunter?"

"Yes. I'm the one who called in the report."

Instead of saying anything, he took out a small pad of paper and a pencil from inside his raincoat and nodded toward a chair. "Detective Meier, ma'am. I've just been combing the parking lot with the men. Why don't you have a seat while we talk about this a moment. We need to fill out a report." He sounded bored, as if he'd been on duty a long time. Before he went on he glanced at the other policeman. "You can go back outside, Tom. I'll take care of things here."

"Did you find the man?" Julie asked. She didn't know which one she was more concerned about, the killer or the dead man. Probably the one who was alive—the one who could come back and kill her.

"No, ma'am, we didn't. There's no trace of either a gunman or a body."

She blinked in confusion. "No body?"

"No, ma'am. No body, no blood, no man."

"But that's impossible!" she exclaimed. "There has to be a body. I saw a dead man."

"I'm sorry, but there's nothing out there now."

Julie felt stunned. Could he be lying to her? But before she could challenge him, Brad Davies came hurrying in the door. Her partner at Lustre, Inc. was tall and darkly handsome, and he knew it. Because of the dimples that creased his cheeks and the black longish hair that fell in an appealing slash across his forehead, women adored him. At one time he'd tried to include Julie in his list of conquests, but she'd found it easy to resist him. She had sized him up and knew he was a sore bet. She had also sized up his business acumen, and knew he was acute on that score. Though sometimes fraught with tension, their relationship ran smoothly for the most part.

"Julie," he said, placing his hands on her shoulders in a gesture of concern as he gazed at her. "The policeman outside told me what was going on. Are you okay, love?"

Brad always called everyone "love." She hoped he didn't try it on one of the policemen, though she suspected he would behave himself. "I'm fine," she answered, "considering everything that has happened. I was really scared. Thanks for coming."

He hugged her. "I can imagine. You must be terribly upset. At least it wasn't a chemical accident. Did you call Roger?"

The other partner in their venture was vacationing in the Bahamas. Roger loved boats, hot sun and aerial acrobatics, which he performed in a borrowed Cessna.

"No, I was too excited to think of looking for his number in my address book. You know, Brad, we should get a silent alarm." They had a system in the plant area in case of an emergency, which notified the reception desk of trouble, and a regular alarm system that could shriek up a storm. But nothing sneaky and ultrasafe like a silent alarm that would alert police to a killer's presence, or an intruder's. "I was so upset I could hardly dial the police. What if George needed help? Or Virgil?" She gestured at the plant manager, a question coming to mind. Hadn't he gone home for the day hours ago? She'd worked past dinnertime, thinking that only she and George were in the building.

It was Brad who verbalized her thoughts. "I thought you went home early, Virgil? What happened, did you circle back?" He used his famous dimpled grin to exude charm and ease.

"I remembered that new recovery process we're considering and came back after dinner to work on it. I wanted to leave it for Miss Hunter for Monday morning, but I fell asleep in the back. Sorry, Miss Hunter," Virgil said, shuffling his feet and looking humble.

Julie waved him off.

"I wish I could have helped. I feel awful," Virgil went on. "You could have been killed."

"I appreciate your concern, but please don't worry about it. I'm fine, and what happened to me was hardly your fault."

"If we could get started," Detective Meier said, drawing them back to the present. He sank into a nearby desk chair and readied his pencil. "I really need to get a report filled out and get back to the station."

Still using his thousand-watt smile, Brad turned to the detective. "This is a Friday night. You must get a lot of calls."

The detective nodded. "Unfortunately." He turned to Julie. "Excuse me, ma'am, but do you think we could get on with the report? What did the men look like?"

Julie shivered. She'd never been very good at describing people, particularly people she didn't want to remember. Her brow furrowed as she concentrated. "The dead man had a wound in his chest. I think his hair was gray. He was tall. The other man was tall, too, and blond."

"How tall?"

She shrugged. "I don't know. Six feet, maybe. Six-one."

"How about him? Did he have any unusual characteristics?"

She tried to picture the killer. "He had a scar on his face," she said. "It ran down his cheek right here, like a knife wound."

"Okay. Good. Can you remember anything else about him? Anything that might aid the investigation?"

What could she say? He looked like a professional quarterback and was very attractive? They'd think her daft. She remembered how his hair had shimmered in the light cast by the streetlamps. "No, just the blond hair, the scar and..."

"Yes?"

"The fact that he was attractive," she told him, hoping that would be enough.

"Attractive? How?"

"Good-looking. Athletic." Her eyes clouded as she tried to articulate her thoughts. There had been something mysterious about him, something that set him apart. But she couldn't find the exact words without sounding mysterious herself. If only the killer had been wearing purple cowboy boots or had had a tattoo or something. Then she'd satisfy the detective. Instead she had to shake her head in frustration. "I'm sorry. I wish I could remember more. Did you scour the trees fringing the lot?"

He nodded. "Yes, ma'am, we looked all over. The squads are still out looking."

Apparently without results. "Didn't you find any footprints?" The grassy ground beyond the parking lot had to be soft. It had been raining all day today and yesterday. Someone had to have run across it, over it, sinking into the earth.

"Nothing distinct enough to get excited about."

She was confused. "But the parking lot—surely there are traces of blood somewhere on the asphalt."

He nodded. "Should be, but if there was any, it's down the sewer drain by now and into the river, along with any other evidence. Like I said, the technicians are testing." He glanced back at her, his face lighting up. "Do you have blood on you at all? Did you touch either man?"

Julie glanced down at her clothes and hands, still stunned. "No. No, I didn't get close enough."

So much for that, she thought as his face fell.

"You say the body was by the curb at the edge of the lot?"

"Yes, where I dropped my keys."

"There's a tree there, isn't there?"

"Actually, there are quite a few clustered together beyond the parking lot." Julie sat in a chair by the desk and glanced back outside. The night seemed almost surrealistic—the glow from the streetlamps, the raindrops glistening on the window....

Brad, who'd been listening patiently, pulled the detective aside. They spoke in low tones for a few moments. Julie frowned as the men glanced at her and nodded. Something was wrong, dreadfully wrong. When they were done the detective turned to the elderly security guard. "Did you see or hear anything, Mr.—"

"Ellsworth," George supplied. "No, I didn't go outside. Miss Hunter left for the evening and then all of a sudden she came running back. She was scared to death, and said she'd seen a dead man and a man with a gun."

"But there was nothing that you could see or hear?" the detective probed.

She could tell the security guard wanted to back her story but couldn't. He shook his head. "No, sir. Nothing." He looked at Julie. "Sorry, Miss Hunter."

"That's fine, George." She could hardly expect him to concoct something. She then introduced her still-confused plant manager to the detective. "Mr. Thompson, anything you can add?"

Virgil shook his head. "Sorry. I was asleep."

Detective Meier flipped his pad closed. "Well, I guess that's it then. I'll let you folks go."

"I'll get Julie home and she can get some rest," Brad offered. "Thanks for coming."

"Wait a minute." Julie was stunned. They were going to dismiss the case? Just like that? "Where are you going? What are you going to do?"

"I have to get back to the station," the detective answered. "I'll be in touch."

"But wait," she said as he started for the door. "You can't leave. I saw a dead man."

He paused. "I know, ma'am. I've taken your report."

She gave a half laugh. "I saw a dead man. I want to know what's going to be done about it."

The detective looked at Brad for a moment, then her. All of a sudden she realized they didn't believe her. "There's nothing I can do about it, ma'am. There's no body."

"But I saw it!" she said. "I *saw* it!"

He nodded again. "Yes, ma'am."

"Dammit!" She jumped up, angry now. "Don't 'ma'am' me. I'm telling you I saw a dead man."

"Now, Julie." Brad stepped forward, trying to soothe her. "Don't get excited. Calm down, love." He patted her on the shoulder, trying to guide her back into the chair. "You're... wet and distraught."

Her hair was curling in tight ringlets around her face. She pulled away. "Don't patronize me, Brad. I'm telling you I saw a dead man and a man with a gun."

"I know, Julie, and the police are doing all they can."

"But I don't understand what's happened. There's no body. There's no evidence of a body. Surely they're missing something."

He patted her shoulder and lowered his voice. "Julie, honey, maybe you've been upset lately. Your parents' divorce, the work here. It's been hard. Maybe you—"

"Maybe what, Brad? Maybe I just imagined what happened outside?" she cut in, gesturing at the glass doors. "Is that what they think? Is that what you think? You think I'm crazy, don't you?" The way they were acting she was beginning to doubt her own sanity.

"Of course I don't think you're crazy," Brad answered. "But consider it, Julie. You've been putting in some long hours, and you know you haven't been yourself."

"Oh, come on, don't give me that garbage. Yes, I've been upset about my parents' divorce, and maybe I've been working too hard, but I'm not given to hallucinations. I saw it, dammit! I'm telling you there was a dead man out there in that parking lot and a man with a gun who shot him."

Brad sighed. He glanced at the detective, who shrugged. "Look, Miss Hunter," the detective said, sighing, "it's not up to me to believe you or disbelieve you. I've taken your report. That's all I can do."

Still his doubt lingered in the air. There were no footprints. No blood. No gunshots reported by nearby neighbors. No gun. And no one seen fleeing the scene. Not even the grass seemed disturbed. It was as if nothing out of the ordinary had happened that night.

Except that a man had been killed and another had gotten away with murder. "You checked everything, including any missing persons' reports?" she asked, worrying her bottom lip with her teeth.

"Yes, ma'am, most everything." He gestured toward the door. "In fact, my men are still out there looking. As for a missing person's report, all we can do is keep our people alerted to the fact that one might come in. We'll post it area-wide, into nearby states. How's that?"

Julie wasn't satisfied. "Assuming one doesn't come in, Inspector, what do you think I saw?"

He shrugged. "I don't know. You could have been frightened by a tree or a passing animal. A dog, maybe? It's dark outside—and stormy. Anything, really."

And her imagination had gone wild? She didn't even fill in his ludicrous suggestion. He seemed so certain, so cut and dry. Could she have imagined the incident, been frightened by a tree? Doubts began to assail her. It didn't seem possible, but she had been working hard, and she was tired. She had to admit she'd been kind of spooked by the weather, going out to her car alone in the dark lot. She'd almost asked George to accompany her. Yet had she been tired enough and frightened enough to imagine a dead man and a killer?

"So what do we do now?"

"The case isn't closed," the detective told her. "We'll keep checking for missing persons, tips, or clues."

"You can check other suburbs?"

"I can check the nation, if you want."

"That won't be necessary," she said, and sighed. She guessed she should feel satisfied by the offer.

"If you like, you can come down to look at mug shots. Maybe you'll find a picture of either man. If it would make you feel better, I could even have a police artist do a drawing from your description and post an APB."

"You really don't think I saw anyone, do you?"

The detective didn't say yes or no. "Dead men don't just walk away, Miss Hunter."

Maybe the man hadn't been dead. Maybe he'd been wounded. Maybe the earth was flat.

Julie sighed again. At least the detective had apologized. He'd been nice in his own way. "Why don't you let Mr. Davies take you home?" he went on in his kindly tone. "Take a nice hot toddy and go to bed."

"What if I'm right and there really was a murder?" she asked.

He smiled. "If you can come up with a body, I can sure book a crime."

"No body, no crime."

"Yes, that's the way it works."

She nodded. Okay. If that's the way it was, that's the way it was. "Do you mind if I call soon to see if you've gotten any new reports?"

The detective pursed his lips, but controlled his voice. "That'll be fine. We'll try to keep you posted, too." The detective held out his hand. "Okay, Miss Hunter, it was nice meeting you."

"You, too." She took his hand, but she had a hard time keeping her expression pleasant. She wanted to scream, do anything to make sure she wasn't sleepwalking. Somehow she got outside the door, briefcase in hand, conducted by Brad. He left her momentarily to ask Virgil and George to close up after the police were gone, then he joined her outside.

"Will you walk me to my car?" she asked.

"I'll go one better. I'll take you home," he said, opening an umbrella.

She shook her head. "No, that's all right Brad. I can drive."

"Now, Julie," he said in the chiding tone a father would use on a recalcitrant child. "Don't be angry with me."

"I'm not angry—yes, I am," she corrected. They reached her car. "And why not? Crazy people are allowed to be mad. That's their problem." She opened the door and threw her briefcase across the seat.

"Julie, please," Brad pleaded. "Come on, be nice. I was worried about you."

She paused, her hand on the door. "I know," she said. "I know you were worried, but I saw them, Brad. I saw a dead man and his killer."

"Oh, love." Despite the umbrella, he managed to take her in his arms and hold her. "Everything's going to be fine. You just need some rest. Let me go with you. I'll get you home and into bed."

She flinched. When would the man give up? She pulled away. "I'll take a raincheck on that, Brad."

"Julie."

"Look, Brad, I'll be fine." Determinedly she smiled again, trying to reassure him. Then she climbed inside the car. "I need to get myself together and figure out what happened here." *And why I'm imagining things—if I'm imagining things.*

He nodded, apparently giving in, and grabbed her hand. "I never could win an argument with you. If you need some time away from the office early next week, let me know. You can have it." He kissed her hand and slammed the car door, then waved and headed toward his own car, parked behind some police cruisers.

Julie wanted to scream in exasperation. It seemed no one believed her. They were trying to humor her, and obviously felt she'd gone over the edge. Rain continued to fall, hammering her windshield in the dark. Even with Brad and the police nearby she couldn't help but glance around, half expecting the murderer to pop out of nowhere. The tall, blond man. Unerringly her eyes went to the empty spot by the gutter. Nothing. Just water gurgling along. How had the body disappeared so fast—in five minutes? What had happened to it? She was fortunate, she supposed, that the police arrived so quickly, though the speed of their response added to the eeriness of the night.

She shivered as she turned her ignition key. The motor roared to life and Julie drove off. As she passed the plant she waved to Virgil, who was getting into his truck. He pulled out behind her, turning left. Brad followed. Then he gunned his black Porsche and squealed from the lot ahead of her. So much for his concern. He probably had a hot date.

She drove east down the road. She kept glancing in the rearview mirror, thinking about the dead man, wondering if every car behind her was the murderer's, trailing her. A few miles later she made an abrupt U-turn ignoring the horns that blared and the brakes that screeched as cars came to a halt on the rain-slick pavement. Dammit, whether they believed her or not, she had seen a body. If she had to find the darned thing herself, or at least evidence of it, she would.

Chapter Two

Lustre, Inc. was located in an industrial park northwest of Chicago. The plant itself was situated on a corner lot, set back from the street, and surrounded by a parking lot on three sides. In order to camouflage all the factories, landscaping had been added throughout the area—large trees, expanses of grass, low, attractive bushes.

Julie parked her car in a row of other cars on a usually busy cross street. Considering the evening's activity, George would probably be more alert to what was going on outside the plant. That is, if he had put on his glasses. Not wanting the security guard to discover her presence and invariably give her a hassle about coming back, she decided to avoid him altogether and walk from the street to the parking lot. Rather, sneak from the street to the parking lot.

After closing, then locking her car door, Julie walked around the red Ford Mustang she drove. Few people were out in the miserable night; only an occasional vehicle splashed by. If possible, the evening seemed even eerier than before. The rain hadn't let up at all, and dense fog had formed a creepy curtain around the buildings. Once she left the street she kept to the shadows, moving slowly toward the spot where she had seen the dead man. She paused near a small bush. Unfortunately she had to step out into the open now to cover the distance between the parkway and the parking lot. She glanced around, looking for passersby. There were none. The police had cleared out, and the plant looked completely deserted.

The only movement was the sway of the trees and the rustle of the leaves in the wind. Rain pelted the ground. A horn sounded in the distance. Almost involuntarily Julie turned toward the factory and the light shining inside. A dim beacon of safety so far away. For some reason she'd brought her purse, and she clutched it to her like a shield as she made her way across the parkway. Not that it would do any good in a confrontation with a gunman. It was large, but it would hardly protect her from a bullet.

There were footprints now, she was sure. With each step she could feel her heels sinking into the soggy grass. It was so muddy that she had to fight to keep her shoes on her feet as she walked, they sank in the mud so. Still she plodded on, finally stepping onto cement. Picking up her pace, she headed across the parking lot toward the trees.

From this distance she could see the spot beside the sewer drain where she had seen the body. There was nothing there now. She clattered to it, disappointed. Kneeling, she closed her eyes, as if this could conjure up the body. But when she reopened them she saw nothing. Water eddied down the drain, swirling away everything in its path. There was no debris, no twigs or fallen leaves, that the police could take in for testing.

Julie sighed. It was so depressing to come up empty. Yet she should have known that finding evidence would be difficult. If the police couldn't find anything, how could she? She stood and glanced into the trees. The leaves still rustled in the night, dark and mysterious. What if something was back there, some proof? The detective had said the police had combed the area, but Julie wanted to make sure nothing had been missed. She started toward the darkened grove, caught by a sound, a movement. Her heart pounded with anxiety, yet she couldn't stop. She had to prove her sanity, if only to herself; she had to find evidence to bolster her case. She stepped closer and closer.

Suddenly, just as she entered the darkness, someone snatched her, and she felt herself whipped back against a lean, hard body. The breath went out of her all at once. Strong arms held her, one hand over her mouth, the other around her waist. "What the devil are you doing back here?" a low, husky voice murmured in her ear. "I thought only murderers returned to the scene of the crime."

What? Was he mocking her? How dared he? She knew without a doubt that the person holding her in a necklock was the blond man. "Please don't hurt me," she cried. "Oh, please. I won't do anything. I promise."

Julie didn't want to die. She still had a lot of living to do. She hadn't climbed the Himalayas or floated in the Dead Sea, two of her goals. Darn, she still wanted to earn an advanced degree in psychology. She wanted a husband. A baby. A family. Hiking boots. God, she was cracking up.

"You know this is really dumb, lady," the man went on, his voice low and rumbling, unnerving her. "Just what are you trying to prove?"

"No—nothing," she stammered, holding very still, waiting for the opportunity to run. "Nothing. I just— I just came back for my—my—" she was having a hard time making something up "—my purse, she finished."

"You've got your purse with you."

"My keys then."

"You're nuts. They were picked up a long time ago."

Didn't she know it. What was she doing here? She should be home in bed, reading a detective novel or working on reports. Calling her mother. Her parents were getting a divorce. After forty years and four children, they were calling it quits. They'd filed briefs in court. Her mother was demanding the stereo. Her father wanted the tool bench. Her sister wanted the blue patterned china. Why was she thinking of this now?

"Okay, listen," the man went on, "I'm going to let you go. Don't scream and don't run. Understand?"

Julie nodded, though deep down she knew she wasn't about to stand there and get killed.

The moment he relaxed his hold, she bolted. Something sparked within her, some instinct of self-preservation, and she tore from his grasp and started to run.

"Dammit!" he swore, taking off through the trees after her.

All Julie could think about was getting away. She ran faster than she had before, harder, knowing that if she didn't make it to the building she would be dead for sure. She didn't bother to scream, not at this moment, not this time. Besides, there was no one to hear her. George was all the way across the parking lot inside the factory, and no one else was around.

But she wasn't fast enough, and her heels made her awkward and clumsy. The man behind her gained on her, then grabbed her again, pulling her back by her collar. "No! Don't!" she screamed, trying to wrench away. "Let me go!"

At first neither of them noticed the car barreling across the parking lot toward them, they were so busy struggling. The headlamps had flashed on when they'd come out of the woods. She broke away again, only to stop dead in her tracks after she turned around and saw the vehicle bearing down on her at full speed. The high beams were on, blinding her, and the tires screeched on the wet pavement. Two streaks of light sliced through the foggy night to form a star-shaped aura. It looked like a picture on a postcard, except that it was real, and it was just a few yards away.

"God," the man beside her murmured. "Quick. Move over here."

Before she knew what was happening she was being dragged behind a streetlight as the car swerved to avoid hitting the pole, barely missing them. As the car skidded away, the sound of its brakes shrieking, the man shoved her over the curb onto the grass. He landed on top of her, and they both sprawled on the ground. "Ouch," she cried. For all her much vaunted education she sure had a limited vocabulary tonight.

"'Ouch' is right," the man said. He tugged her to her feet as he rose. "Come on. We've got to get out of here."

"Please let me go." Julie pulled back, her heart racing with fear. She was so frightened; her mind was knotted up in confusion. She could hear the engine revving and knew the car was circling back, and still she stared at the blond man in front of her. She had to be dreaming, had to be having an awful nightmare. Any moment now she'd wake up in her pink wallpapered bedroom and roll over in bed. "Please don't hurt me."

"Lady, I'm trying to help you. Snap out of it and follow me."

"You can't kill me."

"Oh, please!" He gestured toward the car careering toward them across the black macadam. "I won't have to kill you, lady. If you don't move, and fast, that car's going to do it for me."

Julie turned to look into the dazzling headlights that shot out prisms in the fog. She shook her head, still puzzled. If the killer was here, then... "Who—who is it?"

"How the heck should I know?" the man answered. "I can tell you this much, whoever it is isn't playing games." Grabbing her arm because she was slow to respond, he pulled her with him down the hill.

As she skidded down the embankment, she couldn't help but marvel at the odd turn of events. Instead of trying to kill her, the murderer was now trying to help her.

The ground was slippery, and she fell to her knees at the bottom, mud spattering her face. She was soaking wet from head to toe. Yet she picked herself up and ran, dodging trees and bushes, when she realized the car had jumped the curb, bounced down the incline, then started threading through the trees, still in pursuit. Little sticks, leaves and tufts of grass stuck to her hands and legs at odd angles. If she'd had a mirror she would have sworn she looked like the Creature from the Black Lagoon, encased as she was in a mud-caked raincoat.

Still the man didn't give her a reprieve. "We have to keep running," he panted, leading her along some unseen path. "Head for the creek. My car's parked on the street just across the bridge."

Why was he helping her? "I can't—" She could hardly speak, hardly breathe.

"Don't talk. Just run."

Feeling as though she were still caught up in a nightmare, a terrible nightmare, she concentrated on placing one foot in front of the other and breathing. Her lungs burned from lack of oxygen. Each breath felt torn from her body. Tree limbs scraped her face and thorns pricked her legs. Wet leaves slapped against her body. She could hear the noise behind them, louder. The lights grew brighter as the car chasing them roared through the trees. Then in the distance she caught the sound of sirens. George must have heard the melee and called the police.

But there was no time to wait.

"Hurry," the man coaxed, desperation on his face.

All of a sudden her heeled foot sank and caught in a hole, pitching her forward. Pain shot through her ankle like fire and she collapsed on the ground. "Oh, no!"

He paused. "What's the matter?"

"I've twisted my ankle."

"Damn!" he swore, looking back. The car was swerving around trees and picnic tables, crushing small bushes in its path. The star aura on the headlights looked like the glimmer of death, beckoning them.

"Can you walk?"

"No." She couldn't even stand on her foot.

"Lord!"

"It's coming. It's going to kill us," Julie murmured, watching the car draw closer and closer. She wasn't dreaming. This was real life, death, horror. The front of the car was pointed. It would hit her at chest level, crushing her. A large hood ornament in the shape of a flying woman graced the shiny surface, looking like a statue of the Grim Reaper.

"It's not going to kill us, not if I can help it." Suddenly, leaning down and nearly diving at her, the man hoisted her over his shoulder like a sack of potatoes, then stumbled on toward the creek. "Hang on."

Julie had never been carried by a man before, and certainly not in this position. And definitely not by a killer. The blood rushed to her face and her head bounced against his back with every uneven step. Her long red hair drooped like a soggy blanket. She pushed at him. "What are you doing? Put me down!"

"Want to die?" he yelled out.

She just might if he kept her in this position for very long. But she kept quiet and clutched at his coat as he bounded across the creek and started up the bank on the other side. Just when she thought all the blood was going to cause her face to explode, he turned her right side up and dumped her beside a car. She wanted to faint, but he opened the door and shoved her inside.

When he touched her ankle, she sucked in her breath. "Ouch!" she cried. "That hurts. What are you doing?"

"Trying to get your damned foot inside."

"Where are you taking me?"

"Somewhere safe, I hope."

That was almost funny. How could she be safe with a killer? "Wait a minute."

"We haven't got a minute. Get your feet in," he said, poking at her legs.

Foiled by the creek and the bridge, the car chasing them had stopped and started to back up the hill. "The car—it's leaving," Julie said.

"Just to go around the other way. We've got to get out of here." Setting her foot inside and slamming the door, the man rounded the car, jumped in and started the engine. They squealed from the parking space in one swift motion.

Julie wasn't certain which was worse, the pain in her ankle or her terror. He drove like a being possessed, careering down the street at the speed of light, cutting in and out of parking lots, turning up and down alleys. She gasped and closed her eyes as he rounded a corner on two wheels and headed directly for another car.

Please, she prayed. *Please don't let me die like this.* She was wet and muddy. And so darned scared.

"Damn traffic," the man swore, swerving so abruptly that the car now faced the opposite direction.

She clutched the dashboard and held her breath as he pressed the accelerator and shot forward again like a cannonball out of a cannon. Her fingers trembled and her knuckles turned white as the car bottomed out, hitting bumps and potholes, skimming over the ground at an incredible speed. She felt as though they were on a roller coaster gone crazy as they dipped and swayed and her stomach did flip-flops.

"You can relax now," the man said as they finally merged into busy city traffic and slowed down. "We've lost whoever that was."

Julie let her breath out slowly, but she didn't relax. She didn't think she would ever be able to relax again. Or drive in a car without remembering this ride. She glanced behind them. "Are you sure?"

"As sure as I can be from this distance. He scaled that incline quickly and stayed within a block from us. I think I've lost him now. If I take off again, hang on."

She didn't need to be told. She wasn't about to let go of the car seat, not with him at the wheel. If she had to, she would clutch the leather forever. Thinking about it, she wondered how he had managed to outrace the other car in this old beat-up sedan. The seats were ripped or nicked, and patched with tape. The windshield wipers made a strange clacking noise with each swipe across the windows. The chassis, marred by several dents, had lost its luster long ago.

Where was the man taking her? More important, what would he do with her when he got her there? They were still moving too fast for her to jump out. That is, if she could run. Her foot ached unbearably. She took a deep breath and turned to him, a shadowy blond figure in the dark of night. A *dangerous* shadowy blond figure in the dark of night.

Up close he looked innocent, ordinary enough. His broad face tapered to a square chin, now covered by a light stubble of beard. For some reason he seemed taller than he had earlier, perhaps because he was sitting up close to her instead of crouching beside a body. His hair glinted in the dim light, still wet from the rain.

He must have sensed her scrutiny, for he glanced at her. "Are you all right?"

Considering the circumstances, Julie supposed she was great. "Yes. Yes, I'm fine."

"How's your ankle?"

"It aches."

"We'll get some ice on it soon."

Although she knew deep down that it would be smarter just to sit there and not draw attention to herself, there was so much she wanted to know. She took another deep breath, screwing up her courage. "What—what are you going to do with me?"

"I told you before. I'm taking you somewhere safe." He turned a corner. "What's your name?"

"Why?" Would he kill her after he found out her name, then hide her identity?

He frowned. "It's easier to talk to someone who has a name."

She chewed her lower lip nervously. "Julie. Julie Hunter."

"Well, Julie Hunter, you're in quite a mess."

An understatement. If only she hadn't seen anything tonight. If only she'd gone home early. "What—what's going on?"

"Damned if I know."

"What did you do with him?"

He glanced at her again. "The dead man? I didn't do anything with him."

"Why did you kill him?"

"I didn't kill him."

"You ran away."

"And that makes me a killer?" He stared at her between glances at the road.

"Generally it's fairly damning evidence," she said, knowing her voice was shaking and hating herself for it. "You were bending over him with a gun."

"I was checking to see if he was dead."

Sure. "Then why did you run away?"

"I ran away because you tore off through the parking lot screaming. At first I tried to catch you, to talk some sense into you, but you're a pretty good sprinter, and you outpaced me. I couldn't afford to be caught beside a dead body."

"Why not?"

There was a brief silence before he spoke. "Because it was my gun that killed the man."

The statement was chilling, and at the same time crazily reassuring. Now Julie knew she was right. He was a killer. And she had seen a dead man. "Who—who are you?"

The man reached into the breast pocket of his trench coat. She could see the shiny butt of a gun tucked in a shoulder holster, a deadly gun, and she froze with fear. Any moment now he would kill her, too. Silently she prayed. Why didn't she run?

But he produced an identification case and flipped it open, holding it up for her to see. His picture was on one flap, a small official-looking certificate on the other. "Colin Marshall, Private Investigator," she read.

Questions flooded her all at once. How had he ended up killing someone? What was he going to do with her? How was she going to get away?

"You don't believe me, do you?" he asked.

She fought down her nerves. "No," she said quietly.

"Why?"

"Your ID could be false."

"It's real."

"That doesn't make you a good guy."

"It doesn't make me a crook, either."

It also didn't clear him of murder. But why was she talking to him, questioning him? Now that she had seen him up close and could easily identify him, would he let her go?

The city sped by. They had entered Chicago proper. Against the fog and rain, the amber streetlights cast an eerie glow on the road. Maybe she should just play along with him, ask some more questions. She could find out what was going on, such as what he'd done with the body. Only minutes had elapsed between the time she had gotten back to the building and the time the police had arrived. Five minutes, if she had to be exact about it. Only one person had had enough time to get rid of the body—him. She cleared her throat. "If—if that's the case and you are a detective," she blurted out before she lost her nerve, "then how did the body disappear so fast?"

He glared at her. "Someone took it."

She listened, but couldn't imagine someone coming along and scooping up that poor man, then driving off again. How would the skin feel? Would it be cold and wet? Bloody? The dead man's flesh had been pale and mottled, and his mouth and eyes had been frozen open. She glanced out the car window, trying to erase the image from her mind. "Where would the person have been hiding when you and I met?"

"I don't know. The killer may have been waiting nearby. You're right, the police arrived awfully fast for this city. But enough time went by for someone to come along and pick the body up after we left. They would have had to be quick, of course, but it could have been done. I'd be willing to bet it was the same person or persons who tried to run us down."

He was right. If he was the killer, why would someone have tried to run them down? Still, she had to be careful, and not too ready to let her guard down. Maybe he was trying to trick her for some reason. "Why do you think more than one person was involved?"

"The dead man was big. Whoever killed him was either strong or had a partner. I thought I saw two people in the car following us. By the way, why didn't you move when I asked you to?"

"I don't know. I couldn't." She hadn't been thinking too straight.

"Well, I think they were after me, not you, so I guess it doesn't matter. The bottom line is, you're alive."

"What do you mean, they were after you?"

"I mean the person—or persons—driving the car was trying to kill me, not you."

Nothing made sense to Julie. "And why were they doing that?"

"Why would someone try to kill you?" he countered. "You haven't done anything." He flicked his gaze to her. "Have you?"

Nothing except witness a murder. "Not that I know of."

"So tell me," he said, "what were you doing there? Why did you go back?"

"To find the body."

"You came back to find a body?" he repeated incredulously, looking at her as though she had lost her senses. "You risked your life for a corpse?"

"The police didn't believe me."

"So you came back?"

She knew it sounded stupid, but she couldn't do anything about it now. "Where did you go when I called the police?"

"Down the block to my car."

"Why didn't they find you?"

"Because I moved to a parking lot near another building and watched what was going on from there. Unfortunately I missed what happened to the body. By the time I got my car and reached the lot, the police were scouting the area."

Julie was amazed at how easily he talked. He answered her questions as blithely as if they were exchanging social amenities. "What were you doing there?" she continued.

"Meeting someone."

"No, I mean an hour ago," she said. "What were you doing there then?"

"Waiting."

For what? Her? Had he guessed she would come back? "Who was the dead man, do you know?"

"No."

How could anyone kill a person he didn't even know? Under the right circumstances a crime of passion might be excused, but out and out murder... He had to have planned it. Stalked the man. Shot him. Cleaned up the evidence. Colin Marshall was an imposing man, capable of anything. She shivered.

"Cold?"

"Yes," she answered, although her shudder had been one of fear.

He reached over and flipped on a switch. Warm air blasted her feet. "Better?"

She nodded. "Yes, thank you." She was more wet than anything else. Mud coated her hands and she wiped them on her dress. The green silk was totally ruined now, ripped in places. Her hair still dripped water.

"Does your ankle hurt?"

While her injury hadn't stopped throbbing, it was the least of her worries. The murder was uppermost in her mind. And the murderer. "It's still sore."

"Maybe you ought to take off your shoe."

Then how would she get away? She was planning to run, twisted ankle or not. At the next stoplight she was going to jump out of the car. This was Chicago, after all, the land of Al Capone and questionable politics. There were police all over. All she had to do was flag down a cruiser. Trying to think of how to answer him, she moved her hand to the door handle. "My foot might swell."

"It doesn't work from the inside."

"What?" The low, ominous words made her heart beat even faster, if possible. She paused. How had he known what she was doing?

"The door handle doesn't work from the inside," he repeated, flicking his gaze to her again. "It's an old car." He slammed against the inside of the door with his fist. "Sometimes the windows don't work, either. You have to give them a whack."

She was trapped in his car. Resisting the urge to try the handle anyhow, Julie moved her hand away and rested it in her lap. What if he got angry at her escape attempt? She might be able to run, but she wasn't fooling herself. She couldn't go very fast and there was no way she could match his strength.

But he didn't seem concerned. "You're frightened, aren't you? Why do you want to get away?"

That should have been obvious. "I don't know."

"Sure?"

She shrugged. "I was just looking for something to hold on to."

"You really don't believe me, do you?"

Julie met his level gaze. In the darkness of the car his features were as obscure as they'd been under the streetlight. She felt another shiver of fear. She didn't know what to think. All she knew was that by Colin Marshall's own admission the dead man had been shot with his gun. And she was being held captive in his car. Sure, he'd rescued her from getting mowed down by an errant car in the parking lot. But who was to say he hadn't rescued her for some other purpose, some diabolical scheme? She needed to get away just to think.

Colin Marshall had his own questions. "You think I'm the murderer, don't you? You think I killed that man."

"I don't know what I think," she said at last. "But, yes, I'm leaning toward thinking you killed that man, and have some trick up your sleeve."

He showed her his sleeve. "Empty. See? And I told you I was a private investigator."

"So?" she said. "You could say you're a policeman. That still doesn't exempt you from murder."

"I am a policeman—rather, was a policeman. I'm an 'ex' now. And if we're going to point fingers, you're not above suspicion, either, you know."

Now he was going to shift the blame on her, was he? She watched him as he drove. His hands were sure and he gripped the wheel expertly. He looked in his rearview mirror a lot. Was he always so alert to his surroundings? Or was he looking for the other car? "What do you mean by that?" she wanted to know.

"Why do you suppose a dead man was dumped in your company parking lot?"

She noticed he didn't say *killed*. "I don't know."

"Ask yourself. Why Lustre, Inc.? It's just a small silver reclamation plant, isn't it?"

While it was true that her company wasn't a major force in the industry, it was growing by leaps and bounds. "How do you know about my company?"

"I don't. But I can see its size and I can read the sign emblazoned on the building."

"Oh."

"Besides, I've lived in Chicago long enough to know its basic industries—steel, inorganic chemicals, soap, surgical supplies."

"Sausages."

"What?"

"And sausages. One of Chicago's basic industries."

He burst out laughing, then quieted. "Right."

She saw how his laughter softened the harsh planes of his ruggedly handsome face. Tiny laugh lines appeared, framing a set of deep blue eyes that could dazzle.

"You're gutsy, aren't you?" He couldn't help but admire her. She might be foolish, but she had courage.

"You mean because I'm talking back to you?"

"You think I'm a murderer."

She shrugged. "As I told you, I don't know what to think. And as for your suggestion that Lustre, Inc. is tied into this nightmare, that's ludicrous."

He shrugged. "Believe what you want. But just for the record, I repeat, I didn't kill that man. And you should be wondering why your company's parking lot was chosen for a murder setup."

"Okay. Let's look at your first contention. If you didn't murder that man, who did?"

"I wish I knew."

Julie sighed, totally confused. He was so genuine in his assertion, so convinced. Maybe she was dreaming, after all. It was hard to believe she was sitting there so calmly, her hands folded in her lap, riding along with a possible killer who pleaded innocence. Even if her life wasn't threatened, she'd made a mistake not trying to escape.

She almost laughed. For that matter, she'd made a mistake to begin with by going out the door of the plant this evening. And the day had started on a sour note, which should have tipped her off. Despite the danger she was in, her thoughts drifted to the call she'd received from her sister that morning. Dammit, that china had been a wedding present from her father to her mother! They'd used it only on holidays, every Christmas. Her mother would take it out and wash it so carefully. In all the years not a single piece had been broken. It was like a symbol of achievement, of things that were right and good in the world. Whatever could have happened between them to change all that?

The windshield wipers kept up their clacking vigil, and Julie hardly noticed when Colin pulled into a parking lot beside a high-rise building. "Well, here we are."

She glanced up. "*Where* are we?" she asked, looking around, blinking. If her geography served her right, they were somewhere in the northwestern section of the city.

"My apartment."

This was somewhere safe? "What are you going to do with me?"

He sighed. "Julie, I've told you over and over that I'm not going to *do* anything. How can I convince you?"

She wasn't certain she could be convinced. "If you were innocent you'd let me go."

He paused, then he said, "So far I haven't prevented you from leaving."

She stared at him, not comprehending for a moment. "What?"

"So far—"

"I heard you," she interrupted. "I just didn't understand you. Are you saying you'll let me go?"

He shook his head. "Unfortunately, no. Not now. At least, not yet."

"But why?"

"Because you'd probably go straight to the police, and I can't let that happen. So far they don't have a body, and as long as they don't, I have time to find out what really happened." With that he opened the door to his side of the car and exited. He went around and held hers open in such a polite manner that they might have been courting. "You will cooperate, won't you?"

Julie just kept staring at him in disbelief. How in the world had she gotten into this mess? Worse, this man had the gall to ask her to cooperate, to stand by until he decided she could leave.

"No, I won't cooperate," she said at last, finally gathering her wits about her. "This is ridiculous. I'm not going anywhere with you, and I'm certainly not going to your apartment."

"Just come along, Julie."

"No, I won't come along." Her temper wasn't one of her virtues, and it was rising now, coming to the boil. Her mother used to complain that of all her children, Julie was the hardest to cool once she was steamed up.

"Look," he said patiently, "I realize you've had a traumatic experience and you don't believe me, but I need to find out who killed that man, and I don't have a lot of time to do it in. Please cooperate with me for just a little while."

"And end up locked in your apartment for days—or worse, dead? No, thanks. I don't need to find out who killed that man. I don't care if the police come for you."

He sighed again. "I'm not going to stand here on the sidewalk and argue with you, Julie. First of all, it's raining, and I'm cold and wet and tired. Second, I don't have time to waste. Let's go."

She clutched the edges of her leather seat.

"Damn stubborn female," he muttered. Then before she could object, he stepped forward, grasped her hands and without much effort pulled her free of the car. Then when she tried to resist, he leaned over and hauled her up over his shoulder as he'd done earlier, letting her head dangle down his back. He slammed the car door with his foot and started up the flagstones to the reception area.

"What are you doing?" Julie cried, stunned. "Put me down this minute!"

"Sorry."

"Put me down!" she repeated more forcefully, and started hitting him. "Let me go. You can't do this."

"Why not?"

"It's not legal."

"Men carry women all the time."

"Not like this. Not against their will. This is kidnapping! I'll scream," she threatened. "Dammit!" she shouted. "Help! Somebody help!"

"Calm down."

"No, I won't calm down. Help!" she screamed again. "Somebody help me!" She kicked at him, but he clamped his hands firmly around her legs, entrapping them against his chest, and kept walking forward.

He paused at the door to his building, then opened it one-handed. A man came out the other way. From her position Julie had a hard time making out his features, but he was smoking a pipe, and his dark hair was edged with gray. He was carrying a newspaper under his arm.

"Mister," she pleaded. "Oh, mister, please help me."

"Evening, Colin," the man said, and nodded.

"Arthur. How are you tonight?"

"Great." He peered at Julie and shook his head as if amused, then strolled down the walk.

"Sir?" Julie cried out. "Sir! I need your help." But the reception area door closed, shielding her cries, and the man didn't seem to care, anyway.

When the elevator opened, Colin stepped in and set her on her feet. Forgetting the pain in her ankle, she scampered across the small space and glared at him, her fury charging the air. How dared he toss her around like a rag doll? "You have nice neighbors," she commented sarcastically.

"They are nice, thank you."

Wonderful. He was taking it like a prince. "Why didn't that man stop to see what you were doing with me?"

"Because he knows I'm a solid, upstanding citizen who wouldn't kidnap anyone. He probably figures we were kidding around."

"Oh, sure. Some joke." Julie continued to boil with anger, furious at her inability to help herself. Worse, he was right. His neighbors wouldn't wonder about her at all. Colin Marshall probably had many women visit him, and all the time. Why wonder about one more? In the light of the elevator she could see him clearly for the first time. He was handsome, the type women swooned over. Obviously he was strong and accustomed to having his own way. He had a thrusting jaw—a sign of stubbornness—and a classic profile with full, sensitive lips. His nose was just slightly crooked, and at one time it had been broken. She couldn't help but wonder how. A fight? Then there was the scar down his cheek.

"You know this is kidnapping," she reminded him again, nursing her pique.

"Really? By the way," he went on, "when the elevator door opens you can either come peacefully or I can carry you. It doesn't matter to me."

Julie was so angry she had forgotten her ankle. Now it felt as though it were on fire. The pain radiated up her leg and farther. She gasped. Reaching out, she caught his arm. Rebelling would be futile. She didn't have the strength, and she didn't want another shoulder episode.

He gingerly led her down the hall to his apartment doorway, forcing her to lean into him. A few moments later, as he fished in his pocket for a key, Julie stood rooted to the carpeted hallway floor, petrified. She couldn't help but reflect that she was clutching the arm of a cold-blooded murderer. Worse, she was about to enter his apartment.

Chapter Three

When Colin opened his apartment door and led her inside, Julie almost wished she were back in his arms, even if he was a murderer. A huge dog bounded up to them, barking and looking for all the world like something out of a horror film, a devil's spawn about to pounce. The animal was big and stocky, with a broad chest and powerful jaws. Its shiny black coat was rust-marked over the chest and eyebrows. With its stubbed tail and deep-set brown eyes, it reminded Julie of a fierce Doberman pinscher who would be deadly if provoked.

"Down, Brutus!" Colin commanded, turning to close the door behind them, then drawing the chain lock into place. "Don't worry, he won't hurt you."

Easy for him to say, Julie mused. She wasn't so certain. The dog looked threatening. Its sheer size alone was enough to strike terror into the heart of the most hardened criminal, let alone a lady executive in physical pain. "Shakespeare would be insulted," she murmured, afraid to move. "Is he a rottweiler?"

"Yes. And he's just a puppy." Bending down, Colin greeted the dog with a friendly embrace and a scratch behind the ears. "Good dog. Good boy. Stay down."

Frozen by fear, Julie just stood there, waiting until Colin turned back to her.

"Can I take your coat?"

"What?"

"Your coat. It's wet. Why don't you give it to me and I'll hang it up?"

Julie wasn't planning to stay that long. And why was he being so pleasant to her? Actually, why was she being so pleasant to him? She was being held against her will. But she took her coat off and handed it to him, anyway. The entire time, the dog sat in front of her and whined, watching her with his head cocked.

"He's really anxious to meet you."

As if to punctuate Colin's statement, the animal panted his eagerness. His tongue lolled out one side of his mouth, and he wagged his tail. Posed like that, he looked like a big clown, and not at all dangerous.

But even wagging his tail the dog frightened her. "I don't like dogs," she said. She particularly didn't like big dogs. She'd been bitten once, a long time ago, and she'd been shy ever since.

"He's very gentle."

"He has teeth."

Colin laughed. "Yes, that he does." He gestured toward the other room. "Have a seat."

Julie let her gaze follow his hand. In contrast to his car, Colin Marshall's apartment was almost luxurious. She hadn't expected it to be so attractive. It was certainly nothing like what a murderer would live in. From what she could see, there were several large rooms, with an open area in front of her rambling into a hallway and offset by a galley kitchen to the right. The furnishings were simple yet elegant: thick beige carpeting and several deep cocoa leather chairs and matching leather sofa that sat in a grouping in a sunken living room. Floor-to-ceiling windows lined one entire wall. The bright neon lights of the city flickered beyond. The draperies were beige, to match the carpet, and made from a silky fabric. To break the formal atmosphere, in one corner tall pampas-grass plumes sat in a crockery pot decorated in a colorful Indian design.

She glanced back to him. "Do I have a choice?"

"I'm trying to be nice, Julie."

"Don't put yourself out." Deliberately turning away from him, she started to hobble toward a chair.

"Need some help?"

"No, thank you. I can manage." But with every step she took she grimaced.

"Sure?"

Apparently he realized she was being obstinate. "I'm positive. I'm doing fine."

"I can see that."

Although her back was turned to him, Julie had a feeling he was subduing a laugh. Darn the man! How dared he make fun of her? She gritted her teeth and plodded forward. Unfortunately, adding to her distress, the dog followed, his nails tip-tapping on the floor behind her like a time bomb ready to go off.

Colin didn't bother to pursue the matter. "I'll get you an ice pack for your ankle," he said. "It'll help the swelling. I'll be right back."

As if she'd miss him.

Still in pain, Julie eased into a chair. Her foot hurt so badly she bit her lip to keep from crying. Brutus sat beside her, looking at her and quivering with anticipation. Apparently he wasn't giving up on making friends. She glared at him. "Go away."

He whined and wiggled his body closer.

"Darned dog." Julie held out her hand timidly. "What do you want?"

Which was all the invitation the animal needed. In the space of a moment he was practically nestled on her lap, licking her and whining his pleasure and licking her some more. His tongue tickled. Although shards of pain pierced her ankle at the slight movement, Julie couldn't help it—she laughed. "Goodness, you're aggressive."

He whined again.

"Get down now," she said, pushing at him.

Coming into the room, Colin ordered, "Down, Brutus!" As if shot, the dog curled obediently beside her chair. "Stay boy," Colin said, glancing at Julie. "You have to be firm with him."

She didn't have to be anything with him except angry. But it wasn't the dog's fault she was being held captive. Moving another chair over, Colin elevated her foot on it and placed the ice pack on her ankle. Her innate stubbornness made her want to refuse his help, but stubbornness wouldn't ease the pain and ice would. Walking on her foot had escalated the ache. And she needed relief fast.

"There," he said, "that should do it."

Since he paused, waiting for her response, she had no choice but to say thank you.

"You're welcome." He went over to a closet. "Want something to towel off with?"

Her hair still hung in wet ringlets down her neck and back, and she must have been shivering. "Yes, please."

He smiled, tossing her a fluffy royal-blue towel. "Here you go."

She hated a war of wills. It came packaged with forced civility. Her thank-yous sounded hollow, artificial, but he hardly blinked an eye. "I'll make us some tea in a minute. It'll help warm us both up."

Wonderful. She was chitchatting and exchanging social amenities with a man she hardly knew. A man she worried was a murderer. She felt even stranger being in his apartment, befriending his dog and acting as if nothing were wrong. When were they going to talk? Contrary to what he'd told her downstairs in the car, he was casual, unhurried, as if they had all the time in the world. He took his coat along with hers and hung them in the giant-sized closet. Underneath he wore casual slacks with a white shirt. The stark color contrasted with his dark skin and the bronze hairs that covered his arms, she noted as he rolled his sleeves to his elbows and toweled his hair dry. His hair seemed darker now, too; in the lamplight it glowed a burnished blond, and he slicked it back with one hand.

Julie couldn't help but notice that he was in good physical condition. His movements were easy, smooth, no wasted motions. A shoulder holster crisscrossed his back, and he pulled a gun from it. Then he removed a second deadly looking weapon from the back of his pants waistband and set them both on the closet shelf.

He turned to her. "Finished?"

"Yes." She handed him the towel.

"You might want to get out of that dress," he said. "It's pretty wet. I can loan you a robe."

"I'll be fine." Although she was chilled through and through, she wasn't about to take off any of her clothes. Or sit around in his robe.

Colin shrugged. "Whatever. Just let me know if you change your mind."

Before returning to the kitchen, he flipped on his answering machine and played back his calls. Brutus stayed with Julie as voices filled the air. She trailed her hand along the dog's head and listened, thinking maybe she might get a clue to this mysterious man. The first message was from someone who owed him money and wanted a few more days to pay. Another person thanked him for his deed, whatever that was. Murder? she muted. An attractive-sounding woman seemed quite eager to contact him.

He walked into the room carrying two steaming mugs of tea on a tray.

"Girlfriend?" Julie asked. Although it was none of her business, she was curious.

He shook his head as he handed her a cup. "Sister. Cream and sugar?"

"No, this will be fine."

A male voice was next, breaking an appointment for the following morning. Someone else wanted to meet him to talk to him about a payoff. At that one Julie glanced at Colin, who smiled. "His mistress is blackmailing him."

"I see," she said. More than ever, she was convinced he was a murderer.

"No, you don't." He laughed, guessing her train of thought, and sat across from her, sipping his tea. "Finding it interesting?"

She didn't like it when he made fun of her. "'Interesting' is an odd way to classify murder and kidnapping. How do you rate extortion and blackmail?"

"You don't give up, do you?" Though his voice held anger, she noticed the sparkle in his eyes.

"I don't have reason to give up."

He leaned forward. "Look, Julie, whether you believe this or not, I didn't just bring you here on some whim. Yes, I need you—to keep you from the police—but in addition, you're steeped in danger, particularly now that you're involved. I'm trying to protect you."

"Really? And just who involved me?" she asked. What audacity! she thought. "How in the world can you justify making such a statement? First you force me to witness you standing over a dead man under very suspicious circumstances—"

"I didn't force you to do anything like that. And I repeat, I didn't kill anyone."

"Then you grab me as someone's trying to run *you* down, and force me to get involved in a dangerous chase." She was glaring at him.

"That's right. But if you recall, you were in that car's path tonight, as well."

"So? Didn't you point out in the car that they were trying to kill you, not me?"

"Yes, I did. But I also pointed out that I wasn't sure what was going on, and that now you're implicated. Even if the driver didn't recognize you, I need to make sure Lustre, Inc. isn't involved. If someone is trying to hurt me and you or your company, then being back there won't be safe for a while. Don't you want every stone turned over before you step back into 'civilized' society?"

"Sure. And I want to go on the next spaceship to Mars."

He laughed, relaxing in the chair again, and fixed those dazzling blue eyes on her. "You're one tough lady, aren't you, Julie Hunter? Good. By the time this is over you might need a tough hide. However, I wouldn't discount the Mars trip. Technology may be closer to a voyage than you might think."

Julie wanted to tell him what an exasperating man he was. But just then a voice on the recorder interrupted their conversation. It was the woman again, the one he'd called his sister. She was frantic and wanted to know when he was going to return her call. "Do you know what she wants?" Julie asked.

He nodded. "I gave her kids a cat a few days ago. She probably can't handle a houseload of kids and a wily pet at the same time."

How thoughtful of him. He seemed so amused. "Are you going to call her?"

"No. She'll get used to the ruckus in a few days. It's a kitten, and it can't cause too much damage."

"Why did you give it to them?"

"The kids needed a pet and the cat needed a home."

Julie was amazed. A sensitive private investigator or a complete con artist—which was it? She watched him switch off the machine, then settle into the chair opposite her. He lifted his cup of tea to those—unfortunately—appealing lips of his.

"So," he said, glancing at her, his clear blue eyes making her heart lurch. "Tell me more about Lustre, Inc."

"What do you want to know?"

"Anything. I'm still trying to figure out why someone would be dead in your parking lot."

Her stomach sank. He was still on that. The thought was appalling. "I gather you think that's significant."

"Maybe. Frankly I don't know what to think. I'm grabbing at straws, trying to put something together here. Do you happen to know anyone who drives a cream-colored antique Cadillac?"

"Me? Why?"

"Because that's the kind of car that tried to run us down tonight. Unfortunately, I didn't get the license plate number. We had our backs to the car most of the time."

She shook her head, sighing. "No. I don't know anyone who drives a Cadillac."

"Sure? Someone in your office?"

She frowned. "I suppose someone might have one. It is a fairly common type of car."

"Yes, it is, but the one we saw tonight is an older model, a little more unusual. Do you keep records?"

"At Lustre?"

"Yes."

"Not of cars."

"How many people work for you?"

He was really carrying on about this. "About fifty."

"Shouldn't be too hard to check out. I'll send someone to have a look in the parking lot tomorrow."

"It would be stupid for whoever tried to run us down to use the car they drive to work, wouldn't it?" Julie pointed out. "They could be caught so easily."

"Yes, but sometimes criminals aren't as smart as you might think. Particularly when the criminal is an amateur," he went on, standing up to pour them more tea. At his movement Brutus jumped to his feet and wagged his tail. "Good boy," he said, and the dog settled back down under her hand.

She smiled at the animal and resumed scratching his ears. Aside from being exuberantly friendly, he seemed well-trained and gentle. She could almost forget she was afraid of him. "How old is he?"

"Almost a year. Getting warmer?"

"Yes."

"Does your foot still hurt?"

She moved it gingerly. "Some."

"As soon as the ice numbs it a bit, I'll wrap it for you."

"I'm sure it will be fine."

"You might need a doctor."

She looked straight at him. "I would if you'd let me go."

Colin sighed. "I just don't seem to be making any headway with you, do I? But I suppose from your point of view it would be logical to suspect me."

"From my point of view it's very logical."

"All right," he said, "let's suppose. Tell me, if I'm a murderer or a con man, why did I save your life? I could have run and let the car do my dirty work."

Okay, two could play this game, Julie decided. "But on the other hand," she countered, "supposing you aren't the killer. Supposing someone else is the killer. Why would he try to run us down? All we saw was a body, which is certainly not a reason to kill someone. I thought he just wanted to set you up for murder... why suddenly go for broke and murder you?"

She had a quick mind, he had to give her that. "I don't know... maybe he panicked. But think. Why would anyone *except* the killer try to run us down?"

"Run *you* down. I was merely a bystander," she said. "Maybe someone wants to kill us for a totally different reason."

"And followed me?"

"Yes."

"On the night I committed murder? Okay. That's a fairly big coincidence, but I suppose it could happen. I've heard stranger," Colin said. "Now let me give you some answers for a change. How about if whoever it was tried to run us down for a lot of reasons? First, seeing the body. Second, to shut us up, or simply scare us. Third, out of panic."

She waited for a fourth. But when none came, she asked, "Do you scare easily?"

"No. Do you?"

She was afraid of a lot of things, and nodded. "What makes you think the murderer is an amateur?"

"The way the man was done in. It wasn't a professional hit. They're usually clean—one shot, no blood. The guy must have suffered before he died. Probably drowned in his own blood, from the size of the wound."

Julie flinched at his clinical evaluation, appalled he could be so cool. She fought back the memories that came flooding back and changed the subject instantly. "You said it was your gun that killed him. If you didn't shoot it, how did it get there?"

"Apparently someone stole it."

"Didn't you report it stolen to the police?"

"I didn't know it was stolen. It's an extra gun. I keep it in my office safe. When I got to the plant tonight, I found it beside the body. You're pretty good at grilling a suspect, aren't you?"

She glared at him, ignoring his mockery. "If what you say is true, I would think you'd want to get your version on the record."

"Turn myself in to the police?"

"That's right."

He shook his head, amused. "No way."

"Why not? You insist you're innocent."

He just looked at her. "Truth is a flimsy defense in court, Julie, particularly against evidence. What I have to do is prove my innocence by gathering counterevidence."

"Which is even more reason to call the police. Besides, in America you're innocent until proven guilty."

"Haven't you ever heard of presumed guilty? Or how about circumstantial evidence?" he asked. "You don't seem to understand," he went on. "I've already told you it was my gun that killed the man. Once ballistics are run on the bullet, I'm as good as behind bars."

"But you have the gun, don't you? I don't know much about police work, but on television the detectives can't put a case together without the gun."

"That's generally true. But in this case they can. You see, ballistics have been run on the gun before and are on record."

"You've shot it before?" she asked incredulously.

"Many times. It's an unusual weapon, and it leaves a specific pattern on the bullet. I suspect that whoever the killer is took it from my office safe and used it with that knowledge in mind."

"Why would the killer take the body?"

"I don't know," he answered. "Maybe he has something up his sleeve, some game he's playing, and he's playing it with me. But whatever it is, he's given me some breathing space, and whether that's inadvertent or not, I plan to take advantage of every moment." He stood and checked the ice pack on her ankle. "Feel better?"

Obviously the subject was closed, but his solicitousness was genuine. She wriggled her toe, expecting pain, but her ankle was only stiff. "It feels pretty good, thanks."

"I'll wrap it for you."

He went back to the closet and pulled out an elastic bandage. "Do you want something to eat?"

She wanted to go home, but refrained from reiterating it. She didn't know what to believe at the moment; she certainly didn't want to stay there tonight if she could avoid it. She shook her head.

Without further ado, he put the ice bag aside and pulled off her shoe. His hands were surprisingly strong and gentle, his motions deft as he neatly bound her ankle, working from her foot up. "No wonder you fell." He indicated her high heels. They were the latest style, three-inch spikes. "Do you wear these all the time?"

It was really none of his business. Why did he keep acting as if they were casual friends? "Generally I don't anticipate running down a muddy hill, chased by madmen."

He chuckled, a nice sound to her ears. "These would kill you without running. I'm amazed you don't have more foot problems."

Julie was amazed, too, but not at her shoes. The gentleness of his touch, the way he held her foot cupped in his hand, sent an odd sensation quivering up her spine. What in the world was happening to her? She couldn't be attracted to him, not to a man like Colin Marshall. As he smoothed the bandage, she jerked her foot away, gritting at the stab of pain that shot through her ankle.

"That's good. Thank you."

"Tight enough?"

"Yes." Julie hated attractive men. She hated being attracted to attractive men. They always created such turmoil. In addition, this one was a possible murderer.

"If you aren't frozen by now you should try to keep the ice on it awhile longer. It'll really help."

Where did he get his medical expertise? "Fine."

He turned away. "I'm going to take a shower. Do you want to sleep in the bedroom or on the sofa?"

"I'm not staying here," she blurted. Not now. She was in more danger than ever. Men like Colin Marshall were like the apple in the Garden of Eden—desirable but deadly. She didn't need that kind of trouble in addition to everything else.

"Look, Julie," he said, "it'll just be for a few days, until I can figure out exactly what happened. It'll be to your benefit, too. Besides, I won't tie you up or anything. You're free to move around, make yourself at home."

"Jolly."

"I could make it difficult for you."

"How? What could be worse than being held captive?"

"Being held captive tied up," he answered. "Dozens of other things. You want me to list them?"

"No," she said, paling somewhat. "That's not necessary. Are you...are you going to shoot me?" She hadn't mean it to, but a quaver had crept into her voice.

"Please don't keep pushing me," he said, an angry tone coloring his rumbling voice. "I'm trying to be patient, and I'm not a patient man. Now I'm going to take a shower. When I get done you can let me know where you want to sleep." He turned away.

It took Julie a few minutes to realize he was gone. He had left her. *Alone.* He was showering in the bathroom, which was apparently off the bedroom in the back. Surely he knew she could run. Then again, what if he hadn't thought about it? She could still get away. She could flee!

Holding her breath, she rose unsteadily from the chair. Pain overcame her at the slight movement. She paused, grimacing as she put weight on her foot. As if commiserating, the dog brushed his nose against her hand and whined.

"I'm fine," she whispered to him.

Once her ankle had stopped throbbing, she worked to find an angle that wouldn't send shooting pains up her leg. She located it when she shifted her weight onto the balls of her feet, and discovered she covered ground that way. She could vaguely hear water running in the bathroom two rooms away. Keeping a watchful eye on the hallway, she began to tiptoe awkwardly across the room. All he had keeping her inside was a chain lock and the small tumbler near the doorknob. If she could get to the elevator before he realized she was gone, she could stumble onto the street and flag down a car.

Julie crept toward the door. Jubilation pulsed through her as she got closer and closer. The chain lock loomed in front of her like a giant charm, magnified a millionfold, and her heart thudded so fast she could hardly breathe. When she reached it, she felt instantly relieved.

Then the dog growled.

"Shh," she said to him, but he growled again.

Surprised, she glanced down at him. In the space of a moment the friendly animal had turned into the devil's spawn she had first thought him to be. Big and powerful, he bared his teeth in an ugly snarl and his eyes followed her every move. A low growl rumbled from his massive chest.

Julie didn't know what to do. She stood paralyzed, her hand hanging in midair. Right then Colin stepped from the bedroom. She turned at the sound. He had a towel draped low around his midsection. Soapy water dripped from his hair and ran down his chest, pooling around him on the floor.

"By the way," he muttered, "I meant to tell you, don't bother to try to leave. Brutus won't let you out the door. Rottweilers are natural guard dogs. They'll let you in, but give you a hard time if you try to get out."

Julie just stared at him. She felt fury rising in her. She also felt disturbed by the sight of his bare chest and arms. His muscles were thicker and more corded than she had thought when he was in his shirt, and there wasn't an ounce of fat on him anywhere. Light bronze hair matted his chest, arrowed down his waist and grew heavy on his legs.

Only when he turned around, very pleased with himself, could Julie move. And then it was to ball her fists and nearly throw a tantrum. Instead she hobbled back to the chair, more haphazardly than she had left it, and sank into its cushions, glad to get her weight off her ankle, which was aching horribly. When she managed to gain some control over her reeling thoughts, she reviewed possible escape avenues. Sitting up, she shot a glance at the phone. To her shock, Colin had detached it sometime when she wasn't looking and hidden it somewhere; the answering machine sat alone on the table. The walls looked too soundproof to pound on and draw any attention, and even then, a neighbor would probably think it was Colin and his newest girlfriend, goofing around again. She shifted her glance to the wall of windows. She remembered they were twenty stories up, so unless she could string together a very long line of sheets, she was marooned.

Brutus padded over to her, sat on his haunches and waited. "Traitor," she said. "I thought you liked me. I was starting to like you, you know, but you're no better than a Benedict Arnold. A vicious Benedict Arnold."

He whined mournfully.

She stuck her tongue out at him. "You're ugly, did you know that? In addition to everything else, you're ugly."

When he licked her hand, seemingly apologetic, Julie sighed. He was schizophrenic. Didn't the mentally ill deserve compassion? He was certainly lovable, no matter what. She reached down and scratched his favorite spot, dreading the moment Colin would emerge and she'd have to face him again.

Chapter Four

The next time Colin came out of the bedroom he wore a pair of faded jeans and a T-shirt. The well-worn denim rode low on his hips, fitting his body snugly, and the T-shirt stretched tautly over his broad chest. His wet hair was clean now but all mussed up, tumbling over his forehead. He had shaved. The scratchy growth of beard was gone from his face.

"Would you like to take a shower?" he asked, coming into the room and flipping on the television set. The image of a popular newscaster filled the screen.

"No, thank you."

"You could at least freshen up."

She tossed back her head haughtily. "My, I hope I haven't offended you with my grime."

He laughed. "I'm afraid it would take more than a little dirt to offend me. I've seen some pretty raunchy people in my lifetime."

Julie could well imagine. He was so old, too. And she doubted his life among cutthroats and thieves had shaped the pristine private investigator he proclaimed himself to be.

"You'll be shocked when you look in a mirror," he went on. "I just thought you'd like to be clean. By the way, you can have the bedroom tonight. It'll give you some privacy."

"Gee, thanks."

"You're welcome." He smiled at her again, a quick, amused flash of white teeth. "I'm sorry I don't have any pajamas to loan you, but I assume you'll manage. You can wear one of my shirts. Just help yourself. They're in the closet." He paused. "Oh, I want to wear the white one with the button-down collar tomorrow. Leave it for me, okay?"

Julie clenched the chair tightly to keep from getting up and yelling at him. Why was he goading her? Wasn't it enough that he had her in this position, trapped in his apartment? "Oh, absolutely," she answered, knowing for sure that if she did end up sleeping there it would be in the button-down shirt and anything else she thought he might need the next day. "I wouldn't dream of using it."

"Good. I'm going to scramble some eggs. I'd offer to help you, but I assume that since you got to the front door all right, you can make it to the bathroom yourself."

He was practically forcing her to wash. She would have refused, but after the way he'd carted her in here, he would probably force her to take a shower, too. "I'm sure I'll be fine."

He just nodded, amused by her. She was still acting as though she were mortally wounded. "Take your time." Then he disappeared into the kitchen.

Trying to ignore the pain in her ankle, Julie struggled up and hobbled into the bedroom's bathroom. When she glanced into the mirror, she was appalled.

Her hair fingered up at all angles; the long red strands were matted, so that the clumps of hair resembled overripe straw or undercooked spaghetti, whichever was worse. Her face was just as frightening, dirt specked and mascara smudged around her eyes. She'd lost one of the gold hoop earrings her sister had given her for Christmas. The other dangled from her earlobe like a big, golden globe. If that wasn't enough, her dress was messier than she had thought. It was ripped in the back along the zipperline, and stained in embarrassing places on the front and back. She thought she would not be out of place in a Halloween parade, disguised as either the bride of Frankenstein or Count Dracula's girlfriend.

A shower and a change of clothes sounded like a blessing from heaven. So would a brand-new body, she thought wryly. She ran the warm water and concentrated on getting the grime off her face and out of her hair—with some success. Although she didn't relish using anything that belonged to Colin, she brushed her hair out with his comb. Last, she sponged a wet cloth over her dress and pinned it closed. Nothing fancy, but it would have to do. Just before she left she opened the medicine cabinet and found a bottle of aspirin. She swallowed three of them.

Brutus was nowhere in sight when Julie opened the bathroom door. The dog had followed her down the hall, but scampered away when Colin called to him. She could hear the man who had abducted her in the kitchen. More inviting was the smell of bacon and eggs that drifted through the apartment. If anything could get her to cooperate at the moment it was food. Hunger gnawed at her stomach, and she hobbled across the living room.

The dog wasn't in the kitchen, either. She paused in the doorway. Colin's back was to her. He looked so out of place in the small area, cooking, putting bread in the toaster and draining pieces of bacon on a paper towel imprinted with little images of ducks. Somehow she hadn't imagined that murderers might cook and eat and lead normal lives, let alone buy cute paper towels. Yet somewhere they had to have a mother, a family.

A lover. Julie nearly gasped as she wondered where that thought came from.

"Do I have a scarlet *M* on my back?"

"Pardon me?" The sound of his voice startled her. Odd, it was still so husky and low, like smooth whiskey on the rocks. Fiery, yet delicious. Compelling.

He turned to her. "You were awfully intent on something. I thought maybe I had a scarlet *M* on my back. You know, *M* for murderer."

"Oh," she said, and blushed. She had been thinking more like *A* for adulteress, in reference to herself. Who was married here? she mused. She must be more muddle headed than she had thought, and she shook her head to clear it. "No, I was just thinking."

He smiled and set a plate of eggs on the counter. "About what?"

"Your family."

"Interesting. By the way, you were successful."

"Huh?"

"You look nice." He laughed, referring to her grime. "Want some orange juice?"

No sense refusing. "Please." she glanced around again. "Where's the dog?"

"Gone for a walk." He handed her a large glass of juice as she edged onto a counter stool. "I pay a young neighbor boy to take Brutus out several times a day."

Right then someone rapped on the door. Julie turned, startled.

"Don't even think of it, Julie," Colin told her, drying his hands on a paper towel as he headed for the door. Why was it he could always read her mind? "If you keep on damaging that ankle, you could end up with some serious problems. And I'm not in the mood for your screams. Besides, Todd's just a kid. He wouldn't understand." He flung open the door and said, "Hey, guy. Thanks a lot."

"Sure thing, Mr. Marshall," a young voice answered. "See you tomorrow."

Brutus bounded into the kitchen as happy as a lark, dragging a chain behind him. He set his front paws in her lap, trying to sniff her food. Julie stared at his collar in frustration as he nudged her with his cold nose. All it would have taken was a leash, and she could have gotten away from him earlier.

"Down!" Colin said to him, unsnapping the leash and placing it in the pantry, which he locked. Julie spied his action but realized that without the key she couldn't steal the leash. "Thanks for not saying anything."

She glanced from the dog to him. "It wasn't by choice."

"Whatever. Aren't you hungry?"

She looked at her plate. She was starved. But she was also growing despondent. It had just occurred to her that she wasn't going to get away from him. She pushed the food aside. "No, I guess not."

"Sure? You need nourishment."

"For what?"

"Your ankle. In order to regenerate, damaged tissue needs a good dose of protein."

"Really?" She was tired of his sundry diagnoses. "And just where did you get your medical expertise?"

"Local emergency rooms. A few nurses."

"The ones you've killed?"

He laughed again. "Yes, just before I shot them we discussed anatomy and physiology." He nodded to her plate. "Eat, Julie."

"What if I don't?"

"Then I guess I'll be forced to commit mayhem. Or murder," he added. "How do you want to die? Something quick, or do you want to suffer?"

Julie wasn't certain whether he was teasing her or not. The way he'd delivered the threat, in such a low, deadly tone, confused her. Why did she keep trying his patience?

She picked up her plate. Once she started to eat her mood elevated. She cleaned up every last crumb. Colin had finished before her and he placed their dishes in the sink. Then he stretched and yawned. "We'd better get some rest. I've got a big day tomorrow."

Julie didn't need a speech to know what he planned. "I thought you had to contact some people tonight."

He glanced at her. "I made several calls while you were in the bathroom. Does that exonerate me from murder?"

She flushed at his remark, for some crazy reason feeling foolish at keeping up the accusation. The way he acted, so casual, so *innocent*, she was almost beginning to think she was making things up. She was tired and overworked.

But that wasn't possible. Too much had happened tonight. "No, it doesn't exonerate you."

"Too bad. I was beginning to think we might have made some headway." He doused the light. "Want some help getting into the bedroom?"

"No, thank you."

"I didn't think so. Oh, yes," he went on, brushing past her and heading for the closet. He pulled out some sheets and a blanket and tossed them on the sofa. "Brutus is a light sleeper. So am I. So don't try to sneak out."

More than anything, it was his attitude that drove her over the edge. "I hope that one day someone does this to you," Julie told him, "and then you'll know how it feels to be held captive and not know if the man is a killer or not."

He paused in the midst of making the bed and glanced at her. "You're having doubts? Glory be."

Julie wasn't certain if it was the way he made fun of her or her own frustration, but suddenly she began to cry. Huge, fat tears streamed down her cheeks. "Damn you," she said. "Damn you for doing this to me."

"Oh, Lord!" he muttered, stopping again in the midst of fixing the sofa to glance at her. "I saved your life. Why can't you accept that?"

"Should I thank you? Oh, I'm so grateful," she mocked. "I'm really glad you saved me for yourself. When are you going to do me in? You may as well kill me now and get it over with. It would be much more merciful than dragging it out like this. Feeding me. Talking to me. Expecting me to sleep in your bed. Keeping me captive in your apartment."

"Julie, will you just go to bed?" he asked wearily.

"No, I won't go to bed." She started to limp toward the front door, not caring if the dog tore her to shreds. She would do anything to get away from this man. "Not now. Not ever. I'm leaving."

"What on earth's the matter with you?" he lashed out at her, whipping across the room and grasping her wrist before Brutus could bite her. "Can't you see the dog?"

But something had snapped in Julie and she was hell-bent on defying him. "I don't care about the dog. I don't care about you. I don't care about living or dying. Let me go! I'm leaving."

Unfortunately, as angry as she was, she was no match for Brutus, who scurried ahead of her and bared his teeth at her in front of the door. Her courage and determination failed her.

Colin was behind her, a gentle hand on her arm. "Go to bed, Julie," he said in softer tones. "You can sleep here. I'm using the bedroom. Good night."

Once again Julie sat in the living room and watched him stroll away. She clenched her teeth and blinked back tears. Dammit, she would not cry.

Sniffling, she wiped her hand under her nose and glanced out the window of his apartment at the city. The rain was still coming down slowly but steadily. Had it really only been a little more than four hours ago that she had left her office and stumbled on a dead man, and possibly his killer, in her parking lot? So much had happened. So much that confounded her. How could a madman be so kind?

She would never sleep. But she was so tired she sank onto the couch and dug her head into a pillow. And as she did, she wondered what he was doing. Planning her demise?

Colin jerked the covers down on his bed, hoping he'd scared Julie enough that she would go to sleep. She'd really tried his patience, and while he'd hated to threaten her, she had gotten out of control. As much as he admired her mettle, he couldn't let her go, not after what she'd seen tonight. Dead men didn't talk, but neither did dead women. He was pretty sure he'd been set up, lured to the parking lot by someone harboring a grudge. The only question was, who? The bad weather had to have played a part in thwarting the deal, as had Julie's appearance. In fact, he'd bet she'd really fouled things up. And how deeply mired she was in this mess was anyone's guess.

JULIE AWOKE to bright sunshine streaming into the apartment. At first she didn't know where she was. Then the dog nudged her with his nose, and everything came flooding back—the murder, Colin, last night.

She pulled herself from the sofa, all stiff and achy. Every muscle in her body felt as if it had been folded up and put through a drill press. Her foot throbbed. Brushing her hair off her face with her fingers, she headed toward the bathroom, stepping carefully to avoid acute pain in her ankle. Brutus followed her, an obedient slave. Except that he would tear her to pieces if she placed her hand on the front doorknob.

Colin was nowhere to be seen. The bedroom was empty and the bed neatly made. The bedroom windows faced the city, too, the bright city bathed in morning sunlight. This room was as tastefully furnished and arranged as the rest of his apartment, done in the same hues of brown and beige. He was a good housekeeper. Or he hired one. Nothing was out of place. A clock set on the dresser said eight o'clock. Lord, she could use some aspirin.

She found a fresh toothbrush waiting for her in the bathroom and a note propped against the sink head. "I'll be right back," it read. "Don't try to leave. I think I have a lead, and you'll be safer here."

Right. And the earth was flat.

After Julie freshened up she swept back her now shining hair and approved of the image she saw in the mirror.

Since there was nothing else to do, she hobbled into the kitchen, stifling her grimaces and moans as she made her way there. She may as well cook some breakfast. No doubt the phone was gone. He wouldn't leave her with it. When she limped back to the living room she didn't even bother to look. She did notice that the mugs they had used the night before were cleaned up. Apparently she had slept better than she had thought. If only she could have awakened to discover that she had in fact been having a nightmare.

Photographs of the dead didn't appear in nightmares.

Julie was opening the refrigerator, when she noticed the picture lying on top of a portable file cabinet that Colin must keep stored in the pantry, since it was fixed with a lock. The picture was a good likeness of the dead man. She might not have been able to describe him to the police in much detail, but she would have recognized him anywhere. His features and coloring were memorable enough, even though death had distorted them.

Papers poked out of the file cabinet as if Colin had been in a hurry and had abandoned them after riffling through the files. The photograph lay at an angle. Practically holding her breath, her hands trembling, Julie straightened it. Her heart leaped into her throat, and her breath came in gasps. She peered into the face, a handsome face that stared back at her.

She clutched the photograph in her hand. If she had needed further confirmation that Colin was a killer, surely this was it. God, she was lucky he hadn't tied her up and hurt her last night. Colin had told her he didn't know the dead man, yet he had a photo of him in his files.

Why? More to the point, how was she going to get away? He would be back any moment. Why was he playing with her, toying with her emotions? Surely he wasn't so sadistic as to enjoy tormenting her. Or was he?

Julie put the photograph down and stumbled for the door. Her ankle was more limber, but still painful as she stepped across the carpeting. But she refused to stay around another moment, foot or no foot.

Brutus, always at the ready, rushed to the door ahead of her and bared his teeth. Julie flinched and moved back.

So did the dog, and he lay down, waiting for her.

She sighed.

He wagged his tail.

"You're a pain, you know that?" She stared bleakly at him, trying to think. The leash was locked in the pantry. She'd watched Colin place it there last night. But what if she lured Brutus into a room and closed the door? She'd thought about it the previous night, but Colin had been around. There was also no bedroom door to use, since someone had removed it from its hinges. But she knew from experience that the bathroom door was intact.

Forgetting her ankle, she nearly ran through the bedroom, clapping her hands in excitement. "Come on, boy," she called. "Com on, let's go."

Brutus jumped to his feet and scampered after her.

"Come on," she coaxed, backing into the bathroom. But Brutus plopped to the floor, his body half in and half out of the room as he wagged his tail. Dragon feathers, she cursed. She couldn't close the door. She glanced around, frantically searching for a way to pry him inside. Maybe if she stood in the shower...

Wait, she needed some food. A treat. Perhaps a piece of meat. Last night he'd been interested in her food.

Julie half limped, half ran back into the kitchen and whipped open the refrigerator. As usual, the dog tapped at her heels. She grabbed some bologna and reached into a cabinet for a dog treat. Then she went back to the bathroom.

Evidently Brutus wasn't hungry. He flopped down at the door in the exact spot he had earlier and wagged his tail at her again, a stubby tail at that. He didn't even look at the food, much less salivate.

Julie was willing to try anything. "Come on, boy," she said, climbing into the shower. Trying to stand on the back of the tub, she pursed her lips and made kissing noises at him. If she could get him into the tub she could run out the door and leave him inside, trapped behind the door. "Come on, Brutus."

The little tow-headed boy thought she was crazy. Julie could tell the moment he poked his face around the doorway and looked at her. Of course, a lot of people thought she was crazy of late, so that was nothing new. Although she hadn't caught a glimpse of him last night, she knew without a doubt that he was the same child who had been at the door. Her heart did flip-flops in her chest. How had he gotten in without her hearing him? What if it had been Colin?

"Hi, Brutus," the boy said. "Hi, lady." He smiled at her. "Can I take Brutus out now, or do you want me to do it later this morning?"

Julie's heart kept skipping beats. He had scared the wits out of her; a ten-year-old child had frightened her to death. All she could do was stare at him. "How—did you get in here?"

He held up a key. "I got a key. Mr. Marshall gave it to me so I could walk the dog." He glanced at her with a puzzled frown. "Do you always take a shower with your clothes on?"

"No," Julie said. "Just this morning."

She stepped out of the shower, realizing she couldn't let on that she was being held captive. The boy probably liked Colin. And why not? Colin *paid* the kid.

"But I think I'll skip it now. Where are you going to take Brutus?"

"Just to the park. What are you going to do with the dog treat?"

"I was going to give it to Brutus."

"He only takes treats from me and Mr. Marshall."

"Oh, I see," Julie said. "That must be why I was having problems."

"I'm surprised Mr. Marshall didn't tell you."

"Yes, so am I," Julie answered.

"The only thing he'll take from strangers is licorice. He likes licorice. What about the bologna?"

She glanced at the lunch meat in her hand. "I was going to eat it myself."

"Brutus doesn't like lunch meat."

"Oh." Tossing the bologna in the garbage, Julie followed the child from the bathroom.

"How'd you hurt your foot?"

"I fell down."

"Is that how your dress got all dirty?"

"Yes." She scooped up her shoes as he went into the kitchen, intending to leave the moment the kid took the dog out of the apartment. "How are you going to get the leash? Isn't it locked up?"

"I got a key."

Julie kept forgetting. She paused in the doorway. "Don't you think it's kind of weird that Mr. Marshall keeps the leash locked up?"

"Nope. Brutus would go out with anybody then. He's a rottweiler," the boy added, as if that explained it. "He don't like to let people out the door, but Mr. Marshall trained him to go out with the leash and only with the leash. And that's why he comes with me."

"I see."

"Are you Mr. Marshall's girlfriend?"

"Kind of," Julie lied. "Why?"

"He's got lots of girlfriends. I don't like any of them. You've got really red hair."

"It's all messy," Julie said. Of course Colin had lots of girlfriends. She'd guessed that. The information shouldn't have come as a surprise.

"My hair's messy in the morning, too. My mom always tells me to comb it."

"Mine needs more than a comb. It needs to be blow-dried," Julie said. She wished the kid would hurry so she didn't run into Colin coming back to the apartment. "Ready?" she asked when he finally got the pantry open.

He grinned in triumph as he snapped the leash on the dog. "Ready."

Julie waved at him. "Have a good time."

Heart thudding, she waited until she was sure he was on the elevator before she rushed—or hobbled—out the door. Twenty stories down she limped out into the street, trying to look as normal as possible, and flagged down a cab. She jumped inside.

The driver was a big man who smelled of cigars and sweat. "I knew I shouldn't have stopped. How you gonna pay me, lady?" he asked when she gave him her address. He gestured at her empty hands. "You got any money? A purse?"

Julie hadn't thought about the impression she would make on the world. She'd made an effort to clean herself up, but the truth was, her dress looked a fright. And sometime in the frenzy last night she'd lost her purse. She smiled at him. "Look, I'll pay you when I get home. I've got some money in my house."

He shook his head. "No, you don't."

She had never been very good at lying. Apparently she hadn't improved any. She glanced around nervously. He was wasting so much time. Colin could come roaring up any moment. "Look, could you just drive and we'll talk about it?"

He leaned back in the seat, relit his cigar and glared at her. "I ain't no fool, lady. I don't go nowhere until you show me some money. You running from the cops?"

"Of course not." But she was getting frantic. She had to get away. She'd come this far. She had no doubt he would kick her out the door if she didn't come up with something to pay him with soon. She didn't think he'd want her shoes. Remembering her earring, she quickly unfastened it and handed it to him. "How about this? Is that enough to get you to move?"

"What am I going to do with one earring?"

"You can sell it. It's gold."

"Is it real?"

"Of course it's real," Julie said.

He was scrutinizing the piece with all the attention of a Michigan Avenue jeweler, turning it over in his hands and scraping his nail along the hoop. Next he'd bite it. Fortunately he released the brake and headed out into the traffic. Pulling the meter bar down, he asked, "What did ya say your address was, ma'am?"

The ride to her house took a long time for a Saturday morning. Julie lived just outside of Chicago in a suburb close to the plant. Although she had gotten away, she kept glancing back, expecting Colin to appear at any moment, guns blazing. If he was a murderer he would want to silence her now. She was the only person who could identify him, and she knew his name. Perhaps she should have gone directly to the police, but she wanted the safety of home first.

She was still making plans, when the cab screeched to a halt in front of her door. "Here you go, ma'am."

Last year she had purchased an old, stately home as an investment, figuring she might as well live in a house as in an apartment. She'd spent every dime she'd saved renovating it.

The cabbie looked around with a surprised expression on his face. "Nice digs."

"Thanks. I earned them myself."

"Yeah?" He seemed properly impressed.

"Yeah," she answered as she got out of the cab. She slammed the door and leaned in the front door window. "And by trusting others when they asked for it."

When the cab roared off Julie stood on the sidewalk for a moment, her arms spread wide to the sky as she savored the exhilaration of freedom. She felt as though she'd been locked up for ten years instead of just overnight. She glanced around at the other homes, half expecting the neighborhood to have changed. but the tree out front hadn't grown more than a centimeter, if that, and there weren't any more bushes and fences than there had been the day before. The only reminder of last night's rain were the puddles that remained on the sidewalk.

Smiling, deliriously happy, she staggered up the walk to her house. She immediately went to her extra key, hidden under a rock in a flower bed. By the time she'd rummaged around in the soil, she was dirtier than ever. She had to blow the key off before she inserted it in the door. Glad to be home, she tossed it on a table in her hallway, locked her door and went directly to the kitchen. Even her ankle felt better. It didn't hurt half as much.

Lifting the wall phone to her ear, she started to dial her mother's number, only to drop the receiver a few moments later when she noticed Colin standing in front of her.

She saw his shoes first. She had been looking down at her fingernails, grimacing at the dirt under them, when she spotted the shiny tips of his black shoes. From there her gaze had trailed up his casually clad body to his face.

He was angry, angrier than ever. He stood there with his hands on his hips and ire in his eyes. "Dammit, Julie, why did you leave? I told you not to go anywhere!"

"You," she murmured. "Oh, God, how did you find me? How did you get in here?"

He waved contemptuously toward the front door as he picked up the receiver and placed it back in its cradle. "Anybody in the world could get into your house. The locks are so chintzy they wouldn't keep out a trained monkey. Haven't you ever heard of dead bolts?"

"I live in the suburbs."

"They make them for suburban houses, too. Look, get some clothes. We've got to get out of here—"

"No!" she interrupted, shaking her head. "No, you're not taking me anywhere. I'm not going. I just got away from you." How had he found her so quickly?

"Why do you keep fighting me, Julie?"

"You killed that man," she said. "I found his picture in your files."

So they were back to that. Colin sighed. "For your information, I found that picture shoved under my door this morning," he told her. "Someone slipped it there last night. I went through my files thinking I might be able to connect the dead man to someone I know."

He always had a good excuse. "You killed him. I know you did."

Colin just shook his head and gripped her wrist. "Come on, Julie. We'll talk in the car. We have to hurry."

She jerked away. "No! Don't touch me! I told you, I'm not going with you."

He had pulled her from the kitchen, but she dove back in, lunging for the phone. There was no way he was going to take her with him. Not now. All she had to do was get the operator and scream for help. They could trace the call.

But Colin came after her. Before he could do anything he'd later regret, a knock sounded on the front door. "Julie? Are you there, Julie?"

Immediately she recognized Brad's voice. Grasping her waist, Colin led her toward a window so he could glance outside. She could see beyond the lacy curtains, too. A Porsche gleamed in her driveway.

"What on earth is spiffy Brad doing here?" Colin muttered.

Not wanting to incur his wrath, Julie shrugged. How had he identified her partner, and his personality, by a car? Probably the same way he knew about Lustre, Inc. and where she lived.

"We're going to have to wait until he leaves."

For Julie's part, she hoped Brad didn't leave. Perhaps he had heard the brief spat inside and would call the police. She held her breath as he knocked against the pine frame a few more times, then went around to the back. She would have called out, but she feared that would spell both her and Brad's doom. They could hear him walk around the house to the rear. She didn't want to hope too much. If only he could help her.

Regardless of her caution, Julie felt letdown when she heard the car start and back out of the driveway. Colin let her go slowly. She sat down on the floor and wanted to cry. He was gone. And so was her chance to escape.

"Go get some clothes, Julie," Colin said, "we've got to get out of here."

"You go get the damned clothes," she said. Now that she wasn't fighting or thinking she might get away, her ankle had started to throb all over again. She rubbed it.

He knelt beside her. "Julie? Are you all right?"

"No."

Julie was surprised when he placed a finger under her chin and tilted her face so that she was looking at him. Very gently he wiped away a tear that streaked her cheek. His thumb was rough and scratchy against her skin. "I'm sorry," he said, "I know you're frightened and you don't believe me, but I am trying to help. I keep trying to tell you, you're in danger."

He had a strange way of helping, she mused. She shook her head. "The only person you're helping is yourself, Colin. Nobody wants to hurt me. Except you."

"You're involved now in this, Julie. You can't just walk away from it. Neither can I. This is danger and this is real. I'm fighting you and I'm fighting the person who committed the crime and I'm fighting to find out what happened. I can't do it all. I need your help."

Lord, she was so confused. Why did he have to be nice to her? Surely average everyday murderers weren't like this man. Polite, compelling. Convincingly rational.

"Come on, I'll help you get some clothes." He tugged at her gently and locked arms so she could lean her weight into him. "You'll have to lead the way."

Not bothering to object, Julie walked with him toward her bedroom. It was futile to fight. He wouldn't bend, and her ankle throbbed painfully.

Opening her closet, she selected some jeans and a sweatshirt and got out some underwear. Next she found an old pair of tennis shoes, and set them into her blue canvas flight bag. If she was going to have to go along with him, she may as well be comfortable. She could use a barrette. She started rummaging through a drawer, when Colin grasped her wrist again.

"Come on." Not waiting, he pulled her into the hall. "We've got to get out of here. Now," he said.

Although it was the same old refrain, Julie could tell that something had happened. "What's wrong? Colin, what's going on?"

"Gas," he answered. "I can smell it. Do you have a basement?"

"Yes."

"Is the gas main there?"

"I don't know."

He merely nodded. "Hurry," he said, and shoved her in front of him. "The place is so loaded with gas a spark will send us sky high."

Julie was so frightened she felt rooted to the spot. Gas? How had that happened? What was he talking about, anyway?

Colin gently pulled her along after him. "Wake up, Julie. Let's get a move on."

Perhaps it was fear, gut-wrenching fear at the thought of a gas leak threatening her beloved home, or just the way she tried to run on her injured ankle, but halfway down the hall her foot gave out. "I can't move, Colin. It's painful."

Without further ado, he lifted her in his arms and carried her out the door, which he had flung open. Setting her down, he let her lean against him as they crossed the lawn at a steady gait.

They'd barely gotten past the driveway, behind a protective line of bushes that bordered it, when an explosion ripped through the air. Julie buckled to the ground and Colin covered her body as bricks and mortar and splinters of wood slashed through the air. She buried her head in his chest, trying to avoid the flying debris. Even the ground rumbled and shook like a giant earthquake.

What seemed like hours later, everything settled. Julie looked up. One side of her house looked absolutely normal. The curtains hung in the windows, hardly disturbed. On the other side there was only rubble and a huge crater in the ground. A fire burned at the gas meter, which, ironically, was still standing. Flames lapped upward to the sky.

"Well," Colin murmured from beside her, "if I'm the murderer, how do you suppose I managed that little trick?"

Chapter Five

Someone was trying to hurt her. Heavens, someone was trying to kill her, and it wasn't just the man beside her. Julie lay paralyzed on the ground for a few moments, staring at the flames that licked at the remnants of her home. Everything was burning. In the distance she could hear sirens. A few neighbors scampered from their houses and gathered around the perimeter of her lawn, awestruck.

"We'd better go," Colin said, helping her up. "There's nothing we can do here."

"But the fire department. They're coming." Feeling oddly detached from the situation, Julie gestured down the street. It was as if this weren't really happening to her, as if she hadn't just lost everything she had worked for all these years. It wasn't her house that had exploded and was burning.

"There's nothing left to save," Colin told her gently. He could tell she was in shock. He wished there were something he could do, but the situation was hopeless. "No one's hurt. We have to leave."

Why was he in such a hurry? "Where will we go?"

"Somewhere to talk."

Julie glanced around at her neighbors. More and more people had gathered on her lawn, mesmerized by the fire. "Shouldn't I stay? Won't they know we've gone?"

"I'm sure they won't miss you. The important thing is that we've gotten out alive."

"Surely the police will want to talk to us."

He nodded. "Yes, they probably will, but we don't have time to wait for them."

"Why not?"

"Think, Julie," he said, his tone urgent. "Whoever caused that explosion might be still be around. We need to get out of here before he tries again. He may succeed next time. Let's go."

Though she was still puzzled, Julie let him lead her away. They slipped through the people practically unnoticed. One of her neighbors, an older woman, smiled at her and said, "I'm glad you're okay."

"Thank you," she said.

Another neighbor shook her head sympathetically. "Terrible tragedy. What do you suppose happened?"

"I don't know."

"You'll be all right, won't you?"

Although she nodded, Julie wasn't quite sure about anything at the moment, particularly her state of being. Everything had happened so quickly. Not more than thirty minutes earlier she had arrived in front of her house, jubilant that she'd gotten away from Colin. Had it really only been this morning that she'd tricked the kid and hopped in a cab? It seemed like forever.

Colin had parked around the corner. No wonder she hadn't seen his car. Had he been there when she arrived? He opened the door and gingerly set her inside, knowing her shaky condition at the moment.

Then he went around to the driver's side, climbed in and started the engine. While she waited for him, she glanced down at the unzipped canvas bag she was still clutching in her hands. Funny how she hadn't let go of it. Everything she owned was gone, destroyed, leveled, everything except a pair of blue jeans and a sweatshirt and an old pair of gym shoes with holes in the bottoms.

He pulled the car out into the street. "We'll go back to my apartment so you can change. Okay?"

Julie didn't really care. She nodded as she stared at the items in her arms—at the moment the sum total of her life. That and the tattered green dress she was wearing. She didn't even have her high heels. "I should call my parents," she said. "If someone notifies them of the fire, they'll be worried."

"You can use the phone at my place."

She looked at him, surprised. Why would he do that? Sometimes he confused her. He was holding her captive—or at least he'd come to fetch her, angry at her for leaving. And he was going to let her make a phone call? It didn't make sense. But what worried her most was the explosion. "How do you suppose the gas got turned on?" she asked, her voice almost a whisper it had gone so dry.

He shook his head. "I don't know, but we both saw Brad Davies circling around to the back shortly before I smelled gas."

She turned to him, unable to believe her ears. "Brad? Brad Davies? But that's impossible. Brad wouldn't destroy my house. He wouldn't try to kill me."

"He might try to kill me."

"Why would he do that? He doesn't even know you."

Colin shrugged. "How would I know? But he certainly had the opportunity. He knocked at the door and he went around back. Do you have a rear entrance to your basement?"

"Yes, but Brad was only there a few minutes. He wouldn't have had time to turn on the gas."

Colin was silent a moment. "You may be right, Julie. But it doesn't take long for gas to accumulate to a dangerous, volatile level."

She frowned, thinking of the time span, and pushed her hair back from her face. She should have found the barrette. "We weren't in the bedroom more than ten minutes."

"Right. But if you have a thick pipe, a fairly large basement can fill up in less than five minutes, as I recall. Your house isn't all that big." He paused and glanced at her, worry lines creasing his brow. "What's your relationship with Brad Davies?"

Julie flushed, for some silly reason uncomfortable with the suggestion in Colin's voice. "Nothing. We're just business partners."

"Did he ever try to make it more than a business relationship?"

She winced. "Once. A long time ago."

"You turned him down?"

"Yes."

"Was he bitter about that?"

Was he trying to put Brad in the role of a jilted lover getting revenge? That was almost funny. Anything between them had happened years ago, and Brad had more than made up for a lack of companionship.

"Not if I can judge by the number of women he's seen since then."

"He showed up at the plant fairly quickly last night, didn't he? From what I could see, the police had just barely arrived when he strolled in."

That was true, but Brad lived close by. And she had dialed his beeper. "Virgil was there, too," Julie pointed out.

"Virgil. He's your foreman?"

Julie nodded. "That's right. He's been with us for years."

"Any problems?"

She shook her head. "No. Never. He's great at what he does. He's always concocting new ways to increase productivity while decreasing costs."

"How about personal finances? Any problems with bills?"

"Not that I know of. There haven't been any bill collectors knocking down our doors."

"Tell me more about Brad. I noticed he likes expensive cars."

Brad liked expensive everything, from restaurants to flashy clothes. "He bought that Porsche with his own money. His mother died last year and left him several bank accounts, and the plant does well."

"Nice way to spend money. No investments?"

"I don't think so. He bought a boat once. Only he put it in the name of the company. It's moored in the Bahamas."

"Is that where your third partner has gone?"

She nodded. "Yes. Roger's on vacation there. He has another week left before he returns."

Colin frowned. "He knows how to fly a plane, doesn't he? From what I learned this morning, he owns a Cessna and flew it to the Bahamas. It wouldn't take him long to duck out for 'recreational flying' and return to Chicago. His wife would never know the difference."

Julie looked at him, shocked. "What are you implying? My partners are trying to kill me—and you? Isn't that a little paranoid, not to mention quite a stretch of the imagination?"

Colin studied her. "Look, Julie, you saw Brad snooping around the house. I'm just searching for an explanation as to why your house was earmarked for destruction, and why Lustre's parking lot was chosen as the site for a murder setup. There has to be a pattern in all of this."

Julie glanced down at her clenched hands. "Why?"

"Because," he said, growing impatient, "it doesn't make sense otherwise."

Julie fell silent a moment, fighting back her tears. "I loved that old house," she murmured.

He glanced at her, looking sorry. "You're insured, aren't you?"

"Yes, but there are some things you can't replace."

Colin didn't say anything for a moment. "How about your life?"

He had a point. She could be dead. They could both be dead. "Yes. I suppose I should thank you for getting me out of the house in time."

Colin glanced at her again, surprised this time. "You're thanking me? Even if the explosion was meant for me?" An amused grin spread across his rugged features.

"Yes." Either way he had saved her. Whoever had planned the act would have killed her, too.

Silence fell as Colin checked the rearview mirror to make sure they weren't being followed. Then he sobered suddenly. "How's your ankle?"

By now Julie was becoming accustomed to the continuous ache. "Fine, I guess."

"Does it still hurt?"

"Yes, but I'm learning how to cope with a bum foot, which is a step in the right direction."

He smiled at her. "I bought you something while I was out this morning." He pulled a tube of liniment from his shirt pocket and tossed it into her lap. "When we get back to my apartment, I'll rub some on and rewrap the bandage."

What an odd thing for him to do, she mused. They were nearly back to his place. Julie recognized the neighborhood as they drove through it. "Do you think your apartment is safe?"

"Why wouldn't it be?"

"My house wasn't."

"It's pretty hard to get inside my building," he said. "You have to use a code at the door. And if anyone did get as far as my apartment, Brutus is fairly intimidating."

"That didn't stop the person who delivered the photograph this morning."

"No, it didn't." Colin lapsed into silence. "By the way," he said a few minutes later, "it wasn't very nice of you to trick Todd this morning."

"Did he tell you where I went?"

"No, I guessed. He just told me you were gone when he got back to the apartment."

"Weren't you afraid I'd go to the police?"

"I thought you'd go eventually, but my guess was that you'd circle home first."

"Good guess." She sighed. "How'd you find out my address so quickly?"

"Phone book."

"Of course. Silly me," she said, tapping her brow mockingly. "Does the boy know you kidnapped me?"

"Julie, I hate to split hairs, but I told you before, I'm protecting you at this point."

She almost laughed. Since the moment she'd laid eyes on this man she'd been constantly endangered. Even he had admitted the explosion had been meant for him. She was just an innocent bystander, embroiled in someone else's vendetta. "Where did you go when you left this morning?"

"To my office. I wanted to check on several things."

That puzzled her. "But your files were at your apartment. I saw them. You left them out in the kitchen."

"I was in a hurry. Besides, those aren't my older files. They're on microfilm in my office. The ones I keep at the apartment are copies of my current cases. In my line of work I've learned to have a set in both places."

"Why do you keep them in the pantry?"

"Because it locks and because it's one of the last places anyone would look for something valuable."

"So? What did you find out?" she asked, bursting with curiosity.

"Nothing that makes a lot of sense," he said. "I found out where your third partner now is, and that he's interested in aviation. I also called a police department buddy, who's going to check out several things."

"Like what?" she asked as they pulled into the high-rise complex looming ahead of them.

"Like whether Roger filed a flight plan with O'Hare placing him in the vicinity the day of the murder. Like finding out who owns a cream-colored antique Cadillac. And like whether the dispatcher got two calls the night you phoned in. That would explain why the police responded in an unheard-of record time of five minutes."

Julie pursed her lips, unwilling to argue about his hunches, particularly those about her partners. She didn't have the energy. But she had to concede he sounded more and more like a private eye instead of a con man slash murderer. Colin pulled into his parking slot and Julie started to get out the door, when she remembered the handle didn't work.

"Why do you keep this car?" she asked when he came around and opened it for her. "Nothing in it seems to work very well."

"Just the doors and the windshield wipers are wrecks," he answered.

"And the chassis and the—"

"All right," he said, taking her arm and letting her lean against him as they walked, silencing her. For once Julie didn't object. "But the engine's fairly powerful, which makes the car reliable and fast, and after wrecking a couple of new cars I decided an old one would work just as nicely."

Considering the harrowing ride she'd had with him the night before, Julie had no problems following his reasoning. As she hobbled down the hallway after exiting the elevator, she moved away from him, fearful of his proximity and their intimacy.

Colin didn't remark when she flinched from him, but he was just as glad she'd moved away. Along with everything else about Julie Hunter, he found her highly attractive. Which disturbed the dickens out of him. He didn't have time for a relationship, not in the midst of trying to unravel a murder. Hey, he didn't have time for a relationship period. Nor did he want one. Not with his life-style.

Aside from ignoring her, though, there wasn't much he could do to control his feelings. He had tried to lie to himself, insisting she wasn't his type. Too cute, energetic. But whatever he'd told himself was wearing thinner and thinner by the minute.

Brutus was thrilled to see them. The moment they got in the door, he whined and jumped on them. Julie petted him. "Good boy. Down now."

She didn't have to tell him twice. He flopped on the floor at her feet. Colin closed the door behind them. "What's the matter, boy?" he said to the dog. "Tired?" The rottweiler just closed his eyes. Colin frowned at him and shrugged. "Must not have gotten any sleep last night." He glanced at Julie wryly. "But I guess he wasn't alone. I'll fix us some breakfast while you take a shower. You haven't had one this morning, have you?" he said without waiting for her to comment. "Do you like French toast?"

Actually, at this point Julie wasn't fussy. "Are we going to stay here long?"

"I don't know. I still have things to do, and I don't think it's a good idea to be here, in case our mad explosives expert shows up. As you mentioned, the photo was slipped under the door, which means he knows where we are. I have a hunch about that. But while I cook some lunch and make a call to follow up on my hunch, why don't you freshen up?"

If she hadn't been so grimy, she might have refused just on principle. She didn't like to be ordered about, and truly, she didn't know whether to believe him. The man constantly presented her with conflicting evidence, so that one moment she felt he was guilty, the next innocent. All he had on the side of right were his protests of blamelessness and the explosion. Julie didn't have any more energy than he did, though, and she wasn't certain enough about any of it to continue a discussion. She took her clothes and went down the hall to the bathroom. She had a lot to think about and a lot more to consider, and not very much time in which to do it.

Colin watched her leave the room, limping slightly, her shining red hair tossed back, her head held proudly. So far she'd managed to hold up under the stress of a murder threat, a kidnapping and her house burning. She'd hardly batted an eye. She wouldn't even admit that her foot hurt her, and he knew it had to throb like blazes. What made her so strong? So defiant? Perhaps it was her Irish temper. With hair the color of flame, he had to assume she was Irish. She sure had that proverbial Irish dander, and even less than perfectly manicured, she looked terrific. Dammit, he had a crime to solve! He didn't have time to play lover boy.

All of a sudden Brutus whined. Colin glanced at the dog. "I know you like her. What can I say? I do, too. But just remember how much fun we've had as bachelors."

Colin phoned the reception desk. His hunch bore out. Someone had left the photograph with the building supervisor, attaching a note asking that it be slipped under Colin's door. The supervisor never met the person who made the request, since the manila envelope containing the photo was left at the front desk and a tenant had picked it up and given it to the supervisor for delivery.

Colin hung up, satisfied. Turning to the refrigerator, he began to pull out bread and eggs. "We're going to fix the best French toast this side of Toledo," he said to Brutus.

The dog, still gripped by a strange lethargy, gave a whimpering cry and sprawled on the floor in a semiconscious state.

THE WATER FELT HEAVENLY. Once Julie started washing, she didn't want to get out. She let the shower pound her until she felt she would shrivel into a prune. Even her fingers and toes were wrinkled. Rinsing the last of the shampoo out of her hair, she turned off the faucet.

Apparently Colin liked to sing. The door was closed, and still she could hear him in the kitchen, belting out a popular song. She dried herself and slipped into her jeans and sweatshirt. Borrowing his comb again, she ran it through her hair, disentangling the strands. Since she didn't have any makeup with her, she smoothed some cream she'd found in the medicine cabinet on her face, hoping it would help the scratches left by the trees last night. She smiled at his medicine cabinet, which contained shaving lotion, a mug and razor, a styptic pencil, deodorant, red-white-and-blue striped toothpaste in a press-button container and a gold toothpick. The masculine items gave her a warm feeling. She remembered that her father shaved with a mug and razor. As a little girl she'd sit and watch him, fascinated by his stubbly whiskers. Colin fascinated her the same way.

Quickly Julie scuttled that thought. No sense inviting trouble. Closing the medicine cabinet, she left the bathroom. The French toast smelled almost as delicious as the eggs had the previous evening. When she paused at the kitchen door Colin glanced at her. "The blow-dryer's under the sink."

She tossed her hair back over her shoulder. "It'll dry."

"Is the curl natural?"

She nodded. "To my continuous distress."

He laughed. "My sister has curly hair. She doesn't like it, either."

He had straight hair, Julie noticed, thick and blond. She had an irresistible urge to run her fingers through it, to caress the part that grew longish along his neck. She suppressed the urge immediately, appalled at the idea. "I guess people are never satisfied." she said quickly to cover the blush that colored her cheeks.

"I guess." He glanced at her foot. "Want me to wrap your ankle again?"

They'd come too far for her to refuse. Besides, if she moved away she might stop looking at him. Stop wanting to touch him. "Yes, please."

He gestured to the breakfast counter. "The stools are kind of high. Better sit in the living room. You'll be more comfortable."

"Sure." Hobbling back into the other room, Julie handed him the elastic bandage she'd taken off and occupied a chair by the window. She held out the tube of liniment. "Here's the stuff you bought."

"Did you take any aspirin? I forgot to mention there's some in the medicine cabinet."

"Yes, I already found it."

"Good." Colin pushed the leg of her jeans up and frowned. A bruise had formed now, a bluish hue that discolored the swelling. "Julie, you've got to stay off this. You shouldn't have been walking on it to begin with."

"It wasn't by choice," she reminded him. Most of the time she'd run at his urging.

"Sometimes it wasn't," he agreed, starting to rub the ointment into her ankle. "But there were other times when you could have avoided walking."

Such as when she had run off. She pressed her lips together and concentrated on his firm, gentle touch. He massaged her ankle, then moved up and down her calf. The liniment felt warm on her leg, almost as soothing as his hands. "Feel good?"

"Yes," she murmured. And she was talking about more than the liniment. Little shivers of pleasure feathered up her spine. "But that stuff smells."

He smiled. "The better to make you well."

"Now you sound like my mother."

"Did your mother ever tell you to stay away from dark parking lots after hours?"

"No, never."

"She should have."

She looked at him for a long moment. Her mother should also have warned her about tall broad-shouldered blond men with tilted noses and scars on their cheeks. He had started to wrap the bandage. As before, his hands were deft and sure as they smoothed the elastic in place. And as before, she was terribly disturbed by his touch. She couldn't be attracted to him, not to someone like Colin Marshall. She couldn't allow it. He was the exact opposite of everything she wanted in a man, too stubborn for his own good.

He put her foot down. "Can you get your shoe on?"

"I think so."

"I'll get it."

"I can do it." Still upset by her reaction to him, Julie jumped up, intending to stay as far away from him as possible. "Maybe I'll take some more aspirin, after all. I just remembered it was this morning that I took it."

Colin had stood, too, and he walked toward the bathroom. "I'll get it."

Julie started for the kitchen, but Colin came back quickly, without the medication. He looked angry.

"Why didn't you tell me about the bedroom?" he asked, glaring.

"What's the matter with the bedroom?" she asked. She had to admit she had passed through the room in a daze. But surely she would have observed something out of the ordinary?

He lunged for the windows and wrestled with the drapery cords. "I've got to get the drapes closed."

"But why? What's the matter?"

"Someone's been here. There's a message on the bedroom mirror and the dead man's bloody shirt is lying in the middle of the bed. Brutus isn't tired from lack of sleep, Julie. He's been drugged."

"But—but how?" The dog wouldn't eat anything she'd offered.

"Probably a tranquilizer gun."

She felt numb as she watched Colin pull the draperies closed just in case they were being observed from one of the towering buildings across the way. "Get the dog and let's get out of here."

Julie didn't move. She hadn't called her parents. Once again there was every possibility that she might die, and she hadn't let them know where she was. "Who could it be?" she murmured, still watching him. "Also, how could they get in here before us? We didn't linger after the gas explosion." It sure shot to blazes her theory that Colin was involved. No one would go so far as to write a message on his own bedroom mirror and smuggle in a bloody shirt.

"I don't know. This could mean two or more people are involved. Stay down in case there's any shooting from one of the other buildings. I'm going to report a crime in progress to the police," he said.

Two people? Brad and Roger? Her partners? She didn't like his implication, but she knew this was no time to argue. "I thought you didn't want to talk to the police."

"I don't. I only want to get some cover while we get out of here."

That sounded reasonable. Julie nodded. As he dialed, she asked, "Where are we going?"

"Somewhere safe. After I finish I'll get the leash. Be sure and get a good hold on Brutus."

Julie didn't think there was anywhere safe. Not with a killer pursuing them. What had they done to deserve this?

Willing her feet to move, she didn't have to go far to find the dog. He was sleeping near the sofa. "Brutus! Brutus, come here."

The rottweiler got up sluggishly, obeying her words. Grabbing his collar, Julie crouched and coaxed him into the kitchen, half expecting a barrage of bullets to whiz over her head at any moment. Why not? Whoever had left a message scrawled on the mirror could just as easily shoot through the plate-glass windows.

As soon as Colin hung up he headed for the kitchen, where she knelt, holding Brutus by his neck chain. She'd found the spot where he'd been drugged, a needle mark on his thigh, now a clot of blood. Colin snapped on the leash and pushed her toward the door. "Hurry. They're on their way."

"What are you doing?" He had grabbed a pen and was scrawling a note on a pad of paper. "Trying to throw the police off in case they search the building. Make them believe I'm on vacation. Let's see. 'Keep the place clean, Marcie. See you in two weeks.'"

"Won't the police talk to people in the building, the superintendent?"

"I don't usually see too many people. But at any rate, it will look as if I left for vacation sometime in the early evening, which no one can refute. I don't think the police will think anything's amiss, and they probably won't look past this note. Don't worry. I'll call Todd later so he won't come to take the dog out and maybe get hurt. Quick, grab the photo. We don't want to leave it lying around."

"What about the stuff in the bedroom?" she asked.

"I erased the message. I'll get the shirt." He rushed back and grabbed the shirt. Seeing it, the crime came back to her in vivid detail... the night, the nightmare scene. She practically stumbled over the dog as Colin led them carefully to the elevator, glancing from left to right, making sure no one lurked in the shadows.

When the elevator arrived and they got in, Julie turned to him. "Colin, what did the message say?"

"Forget it, Julie."

She stamped her good foot. "I'm involved, too, and I want to know."

He glared at her, concern on his face. "Okay. It said in red lipstick, 'There's no escape now.' But I don't want you worrying about it, hear? You're with me, and as long as you are, you'll be safe."

Julie felt her stomach fall. The queasy sensation was exacerbated as the elevator plummeted twenty floors to ground level. 'No escape now'? In red lipstick intended to mimic the dead man's blood? A chill quivered up her spine. Meeting Colin, no matter how nice some of the aspects were, had its downside, as well.

"Colin," she asked in as steady a voice as possible in the thickly charged air. "Shouldn't we talk to the police?"

"No," he said adamantly. He banged the elevator button again. "I've told you before, Julie. We can't afford to involve them yet."

"But they'll help us. That's what they're there for."

"How are they going to help us?"

"By investigating the murder—or at least the fire at my house. Someone's getting bolder, and the longer we're in the open, the likelier it is we'll get hurt when he catches up to us."

"I've been around, Julie. All the cops will do is arrest me and let you loose. You'll be exposed."

"But, Colin, you're a private investigator. If you explain that to them and point to some of your police friends, surely they'll listen."

"They have a lot of cases, Julie, and don't have time to do a lot of in-depth investigating. Particularly in this sort of case. It'll be cut-and-dried at first."

"But they don't have a body. Why would they arrest you?"

"Believe me, the moment I'm arrested and the killer hears about it, the body will show up. The body will eventually show up, anyway. Like I said, the family's bound to report something soon. Come on." He tugged her free of the elevator and pulled on Brutus's chain to get his sluggish body moving. "They'll be here any moment."

Colin settled them in a corner of the lobby, which was empty except for an elderly man checking his postal box and a young couple on the couch, too absorbed in each other to pay attention to their surroundings.

Sirens shrieked in the distance and Colin signaled Julie to come up alongside him at the windowed door. He put his arm around her waist as two police cruisers pulled up to the curb and pressed her out the door. They looked like a casual couple out for a stroll with a peculiarly listless dog.

As the police passed, their manner urgent and their attention focused on the building, Julie found her breathing easier. Colin ushered her to his car and tugged on Brutus's chain to get him to speed up. The dog seemed happy enough, though his tail wagged in slow motion.

Julie just stood staring at the open door in shock. Colin had pulled the bloody shirt from his corduroy jacket and shoved it under the seat. He rounded the car to the driver's side. "Julie, go ahead and get in with Brutus. We have to get away. If you don't hurry the police will return."

It didn't occur to her not to go with him. They weren't kidnapper and captive any longer, but two people thrown together on a raft in tossing seas. Once inside the car, she braced herself for another wild ride as they drove out of the parking lot, but Colin drove calmly, pulling into the main street as if he hadn't a care in the world.

She could tell he was on the alert. His face was strained, and his eyes were in constant motion, shifting from side to side. He kept a steellike grip on the steering wheel.

"Seven minutes," he remarked. "Good response time. We aimed for that when I was on the force."

Julie found herself shocked. For some reason his remark that he'd been on the force hadn't registered. Now it did.

"You know," she began, "you strike me as more of a vigilante than a policeman."

"A what?"

"You can hardly blame me," she defended herself when he glanced at her in amazement. "You have to admit you don't exactly play by the rules."

Colin merged into the traffic flowing toward an expressway. "If you're talking about rules that would bind my hands in an investigation, you're right. I don't play by them. I believe in right and wrong, though, and I hate like blazes for the little guy to get caught in the crunch. I don't like criminals being on the streets, and I particularly don't like being set up for murder."

"Doing something illegal doesn't bother you?"

"Sometimes the end does justify the means, Julie. I gather you're still bothered by the fact that I haven't turned myself in to the police."

"I guess I'm puzzled by it."

"There's not much more I can say, except that I don't want to implicate myself in a murder until I can find out what's happening. Call it my need for control, but in any case I'm going to stay on top of this one until the end."

Julie mulled this over as Colin increased his speed up the ramp. When Brutus shuffled to gain a new foothold on the back seat, still weary from being drugged, Julie glanced behind them. "Do you think we've gotten away?"

"Looks like it."

"Could anyone be following us?"

He glanced in the rearview mirror. "Could be, but I'm not aware of it."

"It seems much too easy."

"What? Getting away?"

"Yes. Not having to career through the city to escape something or someone."

He laughed. "Want to go fast for the hell of it?"

"No!" She didn't want a ride like last night's ever again. "Where are we going?"

"Wisconsin. Just over the state line. I've got a cabin there. We'll have time to sort things out."

"How's that safer than your apartment?"

"Not many people know about the place," he answered. "And we have to go somewhere. All we can do is hope."

"What can you do from there? I thought you wanted to get information before the body showed up?"

Colin wasn't planning to work from Wisconsin. He wanted a place for Julie to stay for a few days. He'd either phone, or make a few jaunts into the city to follow up leads if necessary. At the moment the key was safety—for both of them. A home base. By now he was convinced that the murder and everything else that had gone on afterward was a setup aimed at him.

But now Julie was involved. She had accidentally gotten caught up in a revenge scheme, and he was bound to protect her. Oddly, he was enjoying it, more than he wanted to admit.

"Right now I'll use the phone. There are a few people I can call for information. But what we need is a refuge for a while until we can figure out the murderer's next move."

Julie wished there were people she could call to help. The only ones she could contact were her parents or her partners, and they had all betrayed her. Her parents had proven that love was fickle, after all, and not to be trusted. All her life she'd admired them, admired their love, thought it could triumph over adversity, over every stress. What a silly notion. And her partners, from the way events were unfolding, seemed to embrace a shallow loyalty. She felt saddened.

"Julie? We'll be okay," Colin said.

How had he known she was feeling despondent? For some reason the dog poked his head over the seat and placed it sleepily on her shoulder. She started to pet him. Here they were, the three of them, man, woman and dog, going to Wisconsin just like a family off on vacation. Everything seemed so calm, so serene. So normal.

And yet nothing was normal.

Worse, she would be alone in a cabin with Colin Marshall. Although he was protecting her, assuring her she would be all right, with each turn of the wheel Julie felt as if she were just entering the jaws of danger. And not all of it had to do with murder.

Chapter Six

Even though they weren't being followed overtly, Julie was nervous during the ride to Colin's cabin in Wisconsin. He stopped once to call Todd to warn him away from his apartment and any danger that might still lurk there. Since he didn't think she should call her parents just yet, she waited in the car. The entire time she kept looking over her shoulder, wondering who had engineered the attempts on their lives and if the person was going to try to kill again. Someone could be behind them right now, ready to shoot or to cause an accident. She glanced at every driver on the road suspiciously.

Apparently worried about the same thing, Colin took a circuitous route north, turning off the highway as soon as possible and heading down country roads. His cabin was located just outside a small town and hidden by a grove of trees. Few people would come upon it by accident—hunters, perhaps, or hikers. The driveway was more of a path, rutted from the heavy rains that had pelted not only Chicago, but this area, as well, for the past few days.

Colin glanced around as the dense forest enveloped them. "Looks like the coast is clear," he said parking the car. "We'll get settled in and I'll go out for groceries later."

"Don't forget dog food." Julie pushed back the eager dog, who was panting at her shoulder. Brutus had traveled well, finally tiring of the whole business and flopping down on the seat to sleep. She wished she could have felt so safe and secure. Now he was ready for new adventures, and bounced against the door.

Colin grabbed hold of the leash. "How could I forget? He eats enough for a horse. Do you want me to pick you up some clothes or toilet articles?"

"A hairbrush would be nice, and some face cream." She could hardly ask for a nightgown. Fortunately she had remembered to bring her flight bag for a change of underclothes. As he went around the car and helped her from her side, she turned her attention to the cabin, quite rustic looking from the outside. "Does this place have an indoor bathroom?"

He laughed. "Yes, it does. But more important, how do you feel about bugs?"

Although she wasn't given to fits of the vapors, Julie hated insects. She hated the thought, feel and sight of them. She particularly hated roaches, which her mother swore inhabited both fleabag hotels and nice homes alike, no matter how much cleaning they got. Consequently, she had her house fumigated twice a month. Or rather, she'd *had* her house fumigated twice a month. "Like most women, I imagine, I abhor them. Why?"

"This is woods. There might be a bug or two when we go in. Don't worry, though, I have some spray."

"Terrific." What else would he lead her into?

"It's better than being shot at."

"Maybe," she said. "No, you're right. I'll take the bugs."

By now Colin had unlocked and opened the door. Julie had agreed with him about the choice, but she couldn't help glancing around when he led her inside. Thankfully no little brown insects scurried under the baseboards.

Inside, the cabin was just as rustic in appearance as outside, decorated in cedar and stone. The front door opened onto a large room with a fireplace in one corner and a hot tub in the other. The furniture was casual, a tweed sofa and chairs grouped in a semicircle around the hearth. The kitchen branched off to the left and the hallway to the right led to another room. Apparently Colin liked looking outside, for here again one whole wall boasted floor-to-ceiling windows. The afternoon sun filtered through the trees, making dappled shadows on the highly polished oak floor. Julie could see birds flitting back and forth among the trees. A squirrel scampered across the ground.

Brutus ran to the window and started barking. "Are you certain no one knows about this place?" she asked nervously.

Colin had opened the screen door to the patio. A light breeze filtered in, dissipating the slightly musty odor that came from the cabin being sealed up. "Aside from my family and a few close friends, someone would have to search real-estate titles to find out about it. Or else get a copy of my tax bill."

"If someone really wanted to kill you, he'd do that, wouldn't he?"

"Now that you mention it, I suppose so. Seems like a lot of effort, though. I'll check around after we get settled in. I'm sure Brutus will let us know if anyone gets near the door."

Julie smiled at the dog. "He's so busy with the squirrel I wouldn't count on him much. Besides, I thought he let people in, not out."

"Because he's still a puppy he barks at any noise. I don't think anyone could sneak up on us."

"What about the windows?" She nodded to the wall of glass, which made her feel vulnerable.

"It's pretty densely wooded back there," Colin explained. "No one could see us to shoot. But I'll close the drapes just in case. Do you want the bedroom or the sofa?"

He'd asked her that once before. The last time she'd been foolish enough to let her temper get the better of her and she'd spent an uncomfortable night on the sofa. "The bedroom, if there's a bed."

He smiled. He'd been opening the windows, and went to the next one. "There is. How about something to drink? I might have a soda left in the refrigerator from my stay here last week."

"Sounds good." Julie was thirsty from the long ride. "Want me to get it?"

"Sure, if you don't mind. I'll open the rest of the windows."

Since the cabin was small, Julie didn't need directions to the kitchen. Admiring the compact area as she wandered through, she went directly to the fridge. "Do you want ice in yours?"

"I don't think there is any," Colin answered. "Or if there is, it might taste stale."

Julie pulled open the refrigerator door and stood paralyzed on the spot when an arm fell forward, almost hitting her. She gasped with fright, and skittered backward. For a moment she didn't know what to say or do. She couldn't scream. She couldn't make her vocal cords work. All she could do was stare, openmouthed, at the bloody appendage and try not to faint.

She almost lost the battle.

"Oh, please." Closing her eyes, she swallowed the bile in her throat. *Please let it be a dream,* she pleaded silently, clutching the door handle for support. *Please let it be a nightmare.* Yet even as she mumbled her prayer, she knew she was awake. She knew without looking that a body was connected to the hand, and whose it was.

"Julie?" Colin called out. "Is something wrong?"

She didn't answer. She was rooted to the spot, paralyzed with terror.

"Isn't there any soda? If not, I can get some when I go out." Colin came into the room, dusting off his hands. Seeing her and what was beyond her, he stood fixed for a second, then moved forward.

"Good Lord," he said. "Go into the back, Julie."

"It's that man," she murmured.

"I know."

"Somebody put him in there. Someone—" She gagged.

"Please go in the other room, Julie," Colin told her. "Get the leash off the dog. I'll be right there."

She started to back away. "What are you going to do?"

"I'm going to try to take some fingerprints."

"Oh, no, you can't do that." Just the thought was abhorrent, as if he were about to commit some sacrilege.

"Julie, we need to know who this man is." His tone was firm. "We're never going to find the killer if we don't do something to find out." He circled around her and went into the living room, returning with a piece of paper and a felt pen he'd pulled from a desk drawer. He started to color the red ink into the man's fingers.

"The killer's still around, isn't he?" All of a sudden it occurred to Julie that someone had beaten them out at every turn. "He's waiting. The killer was here. I know it. He was here before us. He found out enough about you to know that you own this place."

"All right," Colin admitted, "that's probably true. And the little gifts in my apartment were more than likely calculated to make us come up here and hide— and find the guy. But that's no reason for you to fall apart."

Colin was right. She was falling apart. Taking a deep breath, Julie forced her feet to move, first one and then the other. She leaned against a counter, fighting for control. "Colin, is he frozen?"

Colin shook his head. "I don't think he's been in here long. His skin feels cool, but not frozen. There is some rigor mortis, however." Julie flinched, trying not to imagine. "I need a wet cloth. There's some blood on his thumb."

How could he be so clinical? She turned to the sink, moistening a paper towel, then handing it to him. The expression on her face told him she was still in shock.

"Julie, you're going to have to snap out of it," he said. "I need you to help me."

She knew he was right. She had to pull herself together. But it was so awful. When Colin finished he handed her the paper. Small red dots were pressed across it in a row. A few small sparkles caught her eye. They were pressed to the paper, too, with his fingerprints. "Hold this for me. Don't lose it."

He started to stuff the man's hand back in the refrigerator. "Wait," Julie said. "Where did this silver come from?"

Colin glanced at the paper. "That's silver?"

She nodded. "Flakes, but it's silver."

He picked up the man's hand and examined it again. "It came from under his fingernails."

Julie froze. Was this the crucial link to her company Colin had been looking for? He noticed her demeanor, his square chin tilting as he gave her a crooked smile.

"I don't know the connection to your silver reclamation plant, but this may be what we've been looking for." He paused a moment.

"We should call the police. We have to notify someone. We can't just leave the man here," Julie protested.

Colin sighed, unsure of a course of action. "If I call the police now, you realize I'll be arrested right off. This is my cabin."

She didn't know what to say. She just kept thinking how awful it must be to be dead and have your body tossed around from place to place. "We can't leave him, Colin. What's he supposed to do, stay in the refrigerator?"

He glanced back at the stark, white appliance that sat there so innocently. No one would guess it held a corpse. "All right. I'll call the police. I guess it won't make much difference, anyhow. They still don't have a murder weapon, so at least I'm not dead to rights, and this is a small town. It'll take them a few hours to figure out whose name is on the deed and to find my real residence. And if I'm lucky," he added, "they'll probably check around here first, figuring the victim is from this area. It might take them a few days, and by that time I'll have come up with a way to find out what's going on—hopefully."

Julie didn't understand why he should be so calculating, when the victim had been as enmeshed as they, and had come out the worse for wear. But she didn't say anything and watched Colin go to the phone and dial. A few minutes later he spoke to someone in low, abrupt tones. Then he hung up the phone and grabbed her arm. "Come on. I figure we have less than two minutes. The sheriff's on his way. Brutus!"

At his sharp command the dog came running, leaving the squirrel scampering about on the ground outside minus an eager audience. They picked up their belongings and made for the door.

"Where are we going now?" Julie asked.

"I don't know, but I figure we'd better make a run for the car. In addition to the sheriff, the murderer might be waiting for us to leave and planning to shoot again. I'll go first. When I signal you, head for my side and dive in across the seat. Don't go around the car."

Julie wondered how much adrenaline a body could take without collapsing from an overdose. It seemed to her that hers had been pumping out the fight-or-flight hormone continuously for the past two days. Now her heart started thudding again and her stomach lurched.

"What about the dog?" she asked.

"Don't worry about him," Colin assured her. "I'll take care of Brutus."

Julie watched as he ran for the car, ducking and weaving across the clearing. When he reached the door he whistled. Brutus shot across the yard and leaped into the car, as Colin held the door open for him.

Colin turned to her and gestured. Julie was so frightened, so pumped full of adrenaline, that she hardly felt her sore ankle. She made it to the car in record time, diving in and scooting across the seat in one quick motion.

"Stay down," he told her. He jumped in and gunned the motor.

She crouched on the floor with her head on the seat. It was a good thing. At least she couldn't see how he was driving. She knew it was reckless. She could feel the car fishtailing all over the road, taking curves on two wheels. He was going so fast the scenery passing the side window looked like a solid green wall. She started to pray again.

After several hair-raising turns he slowed down. "You can get up now. I don't see anyone."

She sat up slowly and crawled onto the seat. Her hands trembled in reaction. She couldn't take much more running and being frightened. "What about the sheriff?"

"I'm assuming he went to the cabin by the main road," Colin answered. Colin had taken the back roads out of town. Now he headed for the Illinois border. He had to get back to Chicago pronto and turn the prints in to a friend at the police department. Maybe by nightfall he'd have an identity. That is, if he'd managed to get a decent copy.

He glanced at Julie. "Do you still have the fingerprints?"

"Yes." She had clutched the paper so tightly her fingers had made an indentation along the edge. "What do you want me to do with it?"

"For now you can put it in the glove compartment."

She opened the glove compartment and slipped the paper inside. "Would it do us any good to have the silver analyzed?"

"Would it show anything?" he wanted to know.

"Probably not," she said, realizing that even if it did, silver was silver. "I'm sorry, Colin." Now that the moment was over and she'd gotten over her concern for the dead man, she felt bad about implicating Colin in murder. If the authorities were after him, in a way it was her fault.

"For what?"

"Making you turn the body in. Now you're a suspect for sure."

He shrugged as if it didn't matter. "It was bound to happen sooner or later. You were right. It would have been heartless to leave the man any longer."

"Do you think the sheriff will know we were at the cabin?"

"The windows are open, so he'll likely suspect something. In these small towns they don't have the investigative capabilities of a big city, so he'll be slowed down a bit. What concerns me is that we went through town coming in. Someone might have noticed us."

"Will the police be looking for the car?"

"If they get a lead on it. All we can do is wait and hope."

She thought about everything that had happened. "Will the FBI be in on this now?"

Colin glanced at her. "Why would the FBI be involved?"

"A body was taken across a state line."

"That only applies in the case of kidnapping," he explained. "As long as you don't rob a bank, transport liquor or motor vehicles or run a racketeering scheme and involve yourself in extortion, you're home free as far as the feds are concerned."

It did seem odd. He knew a great deal about laws. "Colin, why did you quit the police department?"

"Too much paperwork."

Julie didn't believe that for a moment. Too much red tape, perhaps, but he wasn't lazy. "How will you contact your friend to give him the fingerprints?"

She assumed he was going to contact someone. Otherwise why would he have gone to the bother? "I'll call as soon as we get back to Chicago and arrange to meet somewhere."

"But where? We can't go back to your apartment."

"I'll figure something out."

"Did you say you had an office?"

"Yes, but I doubt it's very safe, either." Brutus whined just then and shifted on the backseat. Colin looked in the rearview mirror at the animal. "I think the first thing we need to do is find someone to watch the dog. We can't keep hauling him around. I'm going to drop him off at my sister's."

"The one you gave the kitten to?"

"Yes."

"I'm sure she'll be thrilled."

"It'll give her something to do besides complain about the cat," he said. "By the way, I guess I owe you an apology, too."

"Why?"

"For involving you in this mess. I'm beginning to think I should have left you in the parking lot the other night."

"Last night," she corrected. "So much has happened that it's unbelievable, but it was only just last night that I spotted you crouched over a man in my parking lot."

He glanced at her, puzzled. "Whatever. I really think I should have left you."

"I would have died. The car would have killed me."

"Maybe not. Particularly not if the killer was after me. Is there anywhere I can take you? Anywhere that you could go to be safe?"

For the past thirty minutes Colin had been trying to figure out what he was going to do with her. He couldn't drop her off at the police. Even if they had the manpower to offer her protection, what would they protect her from? Elusive killers—since it was now clear more than one person had to be involved—who may or may not show their faces? Her house was gone, and he didn't trust her partners. They might be involved in some way. He felt responsible for her, but there just wasn't anywhere he could take her.

She thought about the places. "I could go to my folks' house, I guess, but I'd hate to implicate them in anything dangerous. They might get hurt. Besides, they're in the middle of a divorce."

"Are they living together?"

"Yes, but they don't speak."

"Seems odd."

"It's even odder that they're separating. I know I'm not a little kid or anything, but it's still hurtful. Do you have parents?"

"Yes."

His amused tone made her feel embarrassed. "I didn't mean that the way it sounded, Colin. I meant are they alive?"

"Yes, they're alive. Golfing every other day."

There was a brief silence while Colin glanced at her with an expression that might have passed for admiration. "You've held up well, considering all we've been through."

"Oh, at the very least I've only been hysterical three times that I can count."

"You do all right," he said. "My sister goes off the deep end if the tag on her markdown clothes is wrong."

Now Julie laughed. "Markdown clothes are important."

"I guess that's true when you've got three little kids and you're struggling to pay off a mortgage."

"Where does your sister live?"

"Just down the road."

Julie hadn't realized they had come so far. He'd turned off the expressway several blocks back, but she'd assumed he was taking a less traveled route. "Are we in Chicago already?"

"What's that old cliché, time flies when you're having fun?"

"Ugh."

"Bad, huh?"

"Awful." Funny how they were getting along so well. It surprised her to realize that he could actually be a nice person. They had entered a residential neighborhood. The houses were all built in a row, set back on neat, green lots. There were few trees. Children played outside. Though newer, the neighborhood reminded Julie of her own. "I wonder if the fire department was able to save anything at my house."

"Do you want to drive by later?" Colin asked.

She shook her head. "No. There's really no need."

"How about your insurance agent? I could take you over to fill out the claim forms."

In the middle of being stalked by a murderer? She smiled at him. "Thank you, but that's okay. I'm sure I can file a claim later. I would like to call my parents, though. I've been meaning to contact them ever since this morning. They're probably wondering where I've gotten to. I should also contact my partners. Brad suggested I take a few days off, but I'm sure everyone's heard about the gas explosion and is wondering where I am. I don't want anyone setting off a manhunt."

Colin glanced at her, a grim look on his face. "Now you're thinking like a policeman."

"Thanks. I guess that means I'm progressing," she said mockingly.

Colin looked almost hurt. "I didn't mean it that way. I just meant that you're willing to cover the bases. We know there is more than one person involved because of how quickly events erupted. They happened almost one after the other. Somehow Lustre's involved, and it's better to play safe—"

"Than be sorry," she finished for him.

"That's right," Colin said. "You might also try to feel out people at Lustre about the explosion, fish for clues... see how they react."

Julie glanced again at the houses. The sky was darkening in the east. Because it was summer the days were longer, but dusk had finally arrived. "Speaking of suspicious," she said, "do you think it's wise to go to your sister's?"

"What do you mean?"

"I realize you want to drop off Brutus, but do you think it's wise to go directly to her house? What if the police are there? If they've put you together with this, even remotely, they could have found out where she lives and be waiting for you. They could have found something at the apartment. Or the killer could be waiting."

"Good point." He started to slow the car. "Maybe we'd better wait and have a look."

"Is there any way you can call your friend at the police department first? You might not know anything about the murderer, but at least you'll know if the police have implicated you."

"You know, you're not just good at this, Julie, you're damned good at it." Colin whipped off a U-turn in the middle of the street. "Let's find a telephone."

They went back the way they had come, and Colin drove to a nearby drugstore and parked the car.

"Want to come in?"

She glanced around at the gathering dusk. She knew it should be the other way around, but she felt safe with him and vulnerable alone. Even with the dog in the car. "Yes, I think I will come." She swept her hair back from her face for the hundredth time. "I can pick up a barrette. Will Brutus be all right?"

"He'll be fine. We'll be just a minute."

She didn't like leaving him. People left dogs in cars all the time, and they suffocated or got stolen or, worse, died of heat prostration. Yet no one would come near Brutus. At first glance, he looked just as fierce as when Julie had first met him. Colin opened the windows slightly.

"Come on, let's hurry."

Julie got a brush to go with the barrette. She felt strange strolling around the suburban drugstore just like a normal patron. Couldn't the clerk tell that she and Colin were running for their lives? They certainly looked odd, she in old blue jeans and limping, he unshaven and making a hushed phone call. He was talking so low she could hardly hear his voice. He reeked of suspicion. But no one seemed to notice. Colin finished, hung up the phone and walked over to her. Steering her to the car, and lifting her when she stumbled once, he helped her in.

"Well?"

He slammed his door and started the engine. "So far the police think I'm in Florida on vacation."

"That's good. Will your friend help us?"

"We're meeting later. I just have to get rid of Brutus."

And Julie. But Colin didn't mention that. He still had to figure out what to do with her. Things were getting far too complicated to keep her with him.

They drove back to his sister's. Though he had assured her no one could be around without being seen in the nearly treeless subdivision, Julie noticed he glanced around as he pulled in the driveway. Since it was totally dark out now, most of the neighborhood children were inside.

"I won't be long." Colin grabbed the dog and bounded up the front steps of an immaculate looking raised ranch home. When the door opened he disappeared inside a moment, then bounded back down without the dog and headed for the car.

A woman stood silhouetted in the doorway, holding the leash.

"Colin!" Quickly she ran down the steps, Brutus in tow. "Colin, come back here!"

Julie saw a statuesque blonde with blue eyes standing on the stoop. She was beautiful, though her features were now fixed in anger.

"Meet my sister, Gayle," he said, and pulled the car into the street.

"She seems angry," Julie remarked, amazed at the scene.

"She'll get over it. She's got a short fuse. I told her to keep the kids close to the house for a few days and to contact me if she notices any strangers in the neighborhood.

"I'm sure that set her mind at ease."

He flashed that white-toothed grin of his, and typically she felt a tug at her heart. "She's a grown-up and can handle it."

Bless younger brothers, Julie thought, fortunately never having had to deal with them. "Will the dog be all right?"

"The dog will be fine. The kids will have a great time for the next few days. The dog will chase the cat and the kids will chase the dog—"

"And Gayle will chase them all."

He laughed. "She's a good sport."

"She'd have to be to put up with you."

"I'm not so bad."

Once a person got used to him, Julie agreed. Unfortunately she was beginning to get very, very used to him. Not wanting to think along those lines, she shrugged and said, "So, since that's settled, what do we do now?"

"Now we go to the police...see what we can do with those fingerprints." He glanced in the rearview mirror. "In the meantime, maybe you'd better fasten your seat belt and grab hold of the dashboard. I hate to tell you, but there's an old Cadillac bearing down on us."

Chapter Seven

The glow from the headlights blurred the car behind them. Julie couldn't see much more than an angled front grille and the statue of a flying woman perched on the hood. But that was all it took to strike terror in her heart. The killer was back, following them. She sat stiffly and murmured to Colin, "What are we going to do?"

"Get away," he answered. "Hold on tight."

"Please don't crash." Julie closed her eyes and swallowed the anxiety that crowded her throat.

Colin didn't seem at all tense. He laughed as he pressed down on the accelerator and skidded around a corner. "You really have a problem with driving, don't you?"

"Not usually." She held on for dear life.

The car tipped again as he went around another corner just as fast. Then just as quickly he slowed. "All clear."

"What?"

"It's over," he said. "There's no one behind us."

Just when she had geared herself up. Julie frowned and glanced back. "You lost him that quickly?"

WOW!

THE MOST GENEROUS
FREE OFFER EVER!
From the Harlequin Reader Service

GET 4 FREE BOOKS WORTH $9.00

FOUR FREE BOOKS
FOUR FREE BOOKS

PLUS A FREE ACRYLIC CLOCK/CALENDAR

AND A FREE MYSTERY GIFT!

Affix peel-off stickers to reply card

NO COST! NO OBLIGATION!
NO PURCHASE NECESSARY!

Because you're a reader of Harlequin romances, the publishers would like you to accept four brand-new, never-before-published Harlequin Intrigue® novels, with their compliments. Accepting this offer places you under no obligation to purchase any books, ever!

ACCEPT FOUR BRAND NEW
YOURS

We'd like to send you four free Harlequin novels, worth $9.00 retail, to introduce you to the benefits of the Harlequin Reader Service.® We hope your free books will convince you to subscribe, but that's up to you. Accepting them places you under no obligation to buy anything, but we hope you'll want to continue!

So unless we hear from you, every other month we'll send you four additional Harlequin Intrigue novels on free home approval. If you choose to keep them, you'll pay just $1.99 per volume — a savings of 26¢ off the cover price. There is *no* charge for shipping and handling. There are *no* hidden extras! And you may cancel at any time, for any reason, and still keep your free books and gifts, just by dropping us a line!

ALSO FREE!
ACRYLIC DIGITAL CLOCK/CALENDAR

As a free gift simply to thank you for accepting four free books we'll send you this stylish digital quartz clock — a handsome addition to any decor!

Crystal acrylic case looks good in home or office setting.

Changeable month-at-a-glance calendar pops out, may be replaced with a favorite photograph!

Quartz movement for exceptional accuracy

Battery included!

HARLEQUIN INTRIGUE NOVELS
FREE!

Harlequin Reader Service®

```
AFFIX
FOUR FREE BOOKS
STICKER HERE
```

YES, send me my free books and gifts as explained on the opposite page. I have affixed my "free books" sticker above and my two "free gifts" stickers below. I understand that accepting these books and gifts places me under no obligation ever to buy any books; I may cancel at any time, for any reason, and the free books and gifts will be mine to keep!

180 CIH RDBC

NAME _____
(PLEASE PRINT)

ADDRESS _____ APT. _____

CITY _____

STATE _____ ZIP _____

Prices subject to change. Offer limited to one per household and not valid to current Intrigue subscribers.

```
AFFIX FREE                AFFIX FREE
CLOCK/CALENDAR            MYSTERY GIFT
STICKER HERE              STICKER HERE
```

PRINTED IN U.S.A.

WE EVEN PROVIDE FREE POSTAGE!

It costs you *nothing* to send for your free books — we've paid the postage on the attached reply card. And we'll pick up the postage on your shipment of free books and gifts, and also on any subsequent shipments of books, should you choose to become a subscriber. Unlike many book clubs, we charge *nothing* for postage and handling!

BUSINESS REPLY MAIL

FIRST CLASS   PERMIT NO. 717   BUFFALO, NY

POSTAGE WILL BE PAID BY ADDRESSEE

HARLEQUIN READER SERVICE®

901 FUHRMANN BLVD.
P.O. BOX 1867
BUFFALO, NY 14240-9952

NO POSTAGE
NECESSARY
IF MAILED
IN THE
UNITED STATES

"I have a feeling he was never following us to begin with. And it was a woman at the wheel."

"You saw her?"

"Just the outline of her hair."

"Did you get a license number?"

"The plates were muddy. I couldn't get a fix on them."

Colin pulled up at a stoplight. Julie studied each car as it came alongside them. She felt almost disappointed. "But that was the killer, wasn't it? Why else would we run into the same kind of car that tried to run us down before?"

"Maybe it's just coincidental."

"Out here in the suburbs? Isn't that a big coincidence?"

He shrugged. "All I know is it's gone, and we have other worries now." He turned onto a busy street headed north.

"Where are we going?"

"I'm supposed to meet my friend in half an hour. We'll find a phone and you can make your calls then. And I suppose we ought to figure out somewhere to stay."

"For the night, you mean?"

"It's getting late. I don't know about you, but I'm tired. I could use a good night's sleep."

How could he sleep, with people chasing them? Julie didn't think she'd be able to rest at all. But she'd thought that the night before, and she'd slept like a log. Although, there hadn't been so many threats on her life at that point. Just Colin—who had generated enough anxiety. She was still worried about being with him, near him. Every time he touched her she felt those same wispy feathers shivering up her spine. And she found herself looking at him often, studying him. Along with his eyes, his lips fascinated her. They were full and soft looking, sensuous. She could imagine what they would feel like on hers, touching, gently caressing, probing hard.

"Julie?"

"What?"

"We're here."

She glanced around. "Where?"

"The park. Is something wrong?"

"No." She'd just been caught daydreaming about him. *Again*. She flushed, embarrassed by her thoughts. Here she was, running from everyone from the law to a killer and thinking about being kissed by a man she'd thought a murderer in the first place and dangerous in the second. She had to be suffering from a fever. Or maybe all the events she'd endured had scrambled a few brain cells. So far she'd been tackled and carried and tossed around like some kind of beach ball. *Something* had to be wrong with her. She was fantasizing about a man who was not only dangerous, but handsome and attractive and the worst possible thing that could happen to her. She didn't need to get befuddled by someone who held clandestine meetings in dark parking lots and had enough girlfriends to form his own little harem.

"Ready?"

Why had they come here? She glanced at the park across the street, a large expanse of green, darkened in most areas by shadows. They were just outside of Chicago. Tall, bright lights illuminated a sandy square where a bunch of children played baseball. Parents and relatives cheered from the sidelines. "Is this where you're meeting your friend?"

He nodded. "His kid has a ball game. You can watch while I talk to Paul."

Watching a ballgame wasn't exactly high on her list of things to do, but she shrugged. What was the harm? It would take her mind off of Colin. "Okay."

He leaned over her and retrieved the fingerprints from the glove compartment. Placing the paper in his shirt pocket, he went around to help her from the car. The evening had grown cool. She shivered in spite of her sweatshirt.

"Cold?"

"A bit. Chicago weather's so changeable. I guess I'm glad it's summer."

"I'd give you my jacket, but my gun would show."

He still wore the shoulder holster, with one gun in it; the other was tucked into the back of his pants. "I know. That's okay. Thanks for the offer."

"Sure." As he guided her across the street he placed his arm around her shoulder. Although it was a polite gesture, meant to keep her warm, she found herself shivering again. And not from the temperature. The man was too virile for his own good. "We'll pick you up something later," he continued. "I'm sure we can find a place to stop and buy you a few clothes."

Every time Julie was reminded of the explosion she realized just how much she had lost. "It's hard to believe my house is gone."

"You have insurance, right?"

She nodded. "It's not the same, though. The house was pretty old. But I suppose there's a way to make a house appear antiquey. You're more modern in style, aren't you?"

"Less clutter," he said. "By the way, how's your ankle?"

She limped only slightly now. "I think it's getting better, in spite of all the walking."

"It has to be the good treatment."

"I'm sure." She smiled at him. "All those nurses you no doubt dated."

He merely smiled, amused by her. She wished he wouldn't grin. Every time he flashed his teeth at her she wanted to melt.

They had crossed the grassy area and were nearing the back of the baseball cage. Colin glanced around as if looking for a trap. So he wasn't so blithe about being recognized. Julie started to pull away as a man extracted himself from the crowd and came to meet them.

"Don't worry, it's all right," he said, tucking her back against him. "I'm just keeping you warm."

That was an understatement. Yet she didn't object. She could feel the heat radiate from his body like a blast furnace on high. She leaned against him, feeling safe and very, very warm as the cool air poured around her.

The man he had called "Paul" was short and slightly balding. He wore Bermuda shorts, a green-and-gold shirt, unbuttoned, and a white baseball cap that said Warriors. He nodded at them. "Evening, Colin. Miss."

Colin squeezed her shoulder. "Julie Hunter, meet my friend and ex-partner, Paul Manning. He's still one of the good guys. You can tell by his white hat."

"Nice to meet you," she said politely, but the man just grinned at her and turned his attention back to Colin.

Taking her cue, she drifted over to the stands and laced her fingers into the fence bordering the field.

Parents and children nearby exhorted the two teams on the field to kill each other. As Colin and Paul talked, she pondered whether this was much of a reprieve from her and Colin's terrifying situation.

"Still a man who attracts the ladies, I see."

"And you're the consummate father, watching baseball in the chilly air at night."

They laughed, accustomed to their barbed exchanges. "At least you can deduct a kid from your income taxes, Marshall. Women just cost, particularly the attractive ones like her. Is she cold or something?"

Colin glanced over and saw Julie hugging her sides now. "Something. So what's the news at the precinct?"

"They searched your place, you know, since you reported a crime in progress. They found the note. They were a little confused by the French toast sitting on the counter, but they figured Marcie must have been having company or something. Fortunately your supervisor was out. Otherwise they would have found out you called him about thirty minutes before someone phoned in the anonymous tip about the burglary attempt. They were most convinced by the calls on your answering machine. I hear there are lots. Maybe you ought to check them."

"Good idea."

"I figured you were in some kind of mess. That's the only time you contact me. What's up?"

Colin reached into his jacket pocket and handed over the fingerprints he'd taken. "Think you could run these for me? I need an ID on them right away."

Paul arched an eyebrow as he looked at the small red dots. "These aren't exactly full-blown prints, Colin."

"Sorry, I had a hard time convincing the guy to cooperate."

Colin could be very persuasive. "Okay." Then Paul nodded. "I'll do the best I can. You owe me, you know, for this and for fifty other fixes I've bailed you out of lately."

"No dinner, all right?"

Paul grinned again. "Margie's run out of exotic recipes." He glanced once more at Julie, approval on his rough face. "But you look like you're doing fine with homemade American."

Colin laughed. "Don't get ideas. Someday I'll explain everything to you. Did you get that other information I asked for?"

"Oh, yeah," Paul said, and pulled a slip of paper from his back pocket. "Like you suspected, buddy. There was a call placed to the police just before another was phoned in that night. The reason they arrived on the scene so quickly is that someone phoned in anonymously and said there was a dead body and a murderer at Lustre. The dispatcher was puzzled at getting another call, pitching the same claim, about five minutes later."

Colin looked serious. "That means I was set up, but the scheme ran afoul. The weather must have slowed up the guys, so they arrived ten minutes after the first call. Julie's the one who put in the second phone call—about five minutes later—and even she wondered why the police arrived after only a few minutes."

"Oh, really?" Paul looked surprised. "You going to tell her?"

"Maybe. What bothers me now is why that parking lot was chosen. Is Lustre involved?"

Paul shrugged, at a loss for words. "Beats me. That's your problem, friend. I've got a game to get back to."

"No problem. Will you get those prints in to the station tonight?"

"Yeah. I'll get them on the computer right after the game."

"If you can get something on the old Cadillac and the airport flight path filed by Roger Perry, let me know, too. Call my machine. I'll play it back. But I'll also try to reach you."

"Sure." You still want me to see if the Cadillac is registered to either Roger or Brad Davis?"

"Yeah. And speed it up if you can."

Paul lifted his arms as if in resignation. "You know it's the weekend. And tomorrow's Sunday, which doesn't help matters."

As Paul and Julie passed each other, they nodded at each other. She had decided a Little League baseball game was preferable to returning to the mess she was in with Colin. "Well?" she asked as Colin steered her to the car and helped her in.

"Well, he'll take the fingerprints tonight. He also found a gem. There were two phone calls Friday—yours and an anonymous tipster's both claiming the same thing, that there was a killer and a body in the parking lot. Yours came in about four to five minutes later."

Julie sank into her seat, already tired. "So it was a setup. No wonder the police arrived so quickly."

"That's right." Colin glanced down at her. In the darkness she looked so elusive, like a mirage that might disappear at any moment. How he wanted to hold her, take her into his arms and keep her from flying away. That night he'd watched her in the parking lot, she'd looked much the way she did now, soft, warm, vulnerable. Frightened. Her red hair reflected the light like flames. It was true that so far he hadn't found anyone he wanted to be with, but now things were different. Julie Hunter might be the one woman to change his mind about marriage. She was different. He knew he could care for her a great deal. And he hadn't even kissed her. Yet. Hardly a good thing to admit. Or even to think. Not with the cops and murderers after them.

But he couldn't hold back his thoughts. "Do you have a boyfriend?"

She glanced at him, surprised. "No. I swore off men after I got dumped by a man I thought I loved."

"Just one experience? That bad, huh?"

She shrugged and turned back to look out the front window as he drove. One part of her wondered why she should tell him the intimate details of her personal life, while the other part of her just rambled on. It seemed natural to speak with him, share with him. "I always tell myself that breaking off with the guy was nothing," she said. "And truly I don't care for him now. But if I were to admit the truth, I'd have to say it was painful. He was my first love."

Colin smiled. "They're always the worst, aren't they? My first love was a high-school girl."

"Really? A cheerleader?"

He nodded. "Pom-pom girl. She didn't even know I existed."

If he looked anything like he did now, how could anyone not have noticed him? "Oh, too bad."

He laughed again. "I survived."

He more than survived, Julie thought, if the women in his life were any indication. He'd triumphed.

"Are you hungry?" he went on after a bit. "I think there's a nice restaurant down the block."

"Do you think it's safe to stop and eat?" Doing mundane things like eating and sleeping in the midst of a crisis seemed odd to Julie. They should be running for their lives, or at least investigating the crime.

"We're entitled to food, and we stopped at a baseball game," Colin pointed out.

That was true. But they'd stopped for a contact, not nourishment. Yet people ate and slept all the time, crisis or not. And she was hungry. No, she was starved. The last food she'd eaten were the eggs he'd scrambled last night. The French toast he'd fixed this morning was probably still sitting on his counter, untouched.

Totally unconcerned, Colin didn't even glance at the other cars when he pulled into the restaurant parking lot. Julie kept thinking that the Cadillac might still be around, following them. Who did it belong to? They'd never gotten to her office files to check if anyone in her company owned one. It seemed as if all they'd done was run from one place to the next, trying to stay alive—a rather high priority, she had to admit.

Colin slung his arm around her again to keep her warm as they walked to the restaurant door. It was an ordinary suburban café, complete with hothouse plants, a dessert bar and a pay phone. He nodded toward the phone. "Maybe you ought to make your calls now. We might not get to another phone until late."

"Good idea." But when Julie went to the phone she just stood there and looked at it. She didn't have any change. She didn't have anything.

As if reading her mind, Colin reached into his pocket and handed her several quarters. "Here. I keep forgetting you lost your belongings."

"So do I," she said. "I had to trade an earring for the cab ride this morning.

"The guy took it?"

"Sure, it was gold."

He laughed. "You always surprise me, Julie. You're awfully ingenious."

Although he had an odd way of paying compliments, she basked in his admiration. "Thanks."

"Want me to stay?" The hostess wanted to seat them and had beckoned.

"Why?" Instantly she was on the alert. She glanced out at the lights in the parking lot, at the cars turning in. "Is something wrong?"

"No, everything's fine," he said. "Relax."

As if she could.

"I just want to keep an eye on you. I don't want you in danger."

She was already in danger. Aside from the physical danger, it occurred to her that every moment she spent with him she risked losing her heart to him. "You know, you're awfully nice."

"What?" He stared at her with his mouth open.

Julie was just as stunned as he was by her statement. She flushed. "Never mind."

He laughed and pushed a stray lock of hair from her face. "Make your calls, Julie. Be sure and tell your partners you're fine. I'll get us something to eat."

Julie watched him walk across the restaurant and sit in a booth where he could see her. Not wanting to think about the situation—or her attraction to him—she turned to the phone.

Her mother answered on the first ring. Colleen Hunter was thrilled to hear from her daughter. "Your father and I have been worried sick about you. The police called early this morning and we've been trying to find you ever since. They want to talk to you about your house. You know it exploded."

"Yes, I know, Mom. I'm fine. I'm sorry I worried you."

"They say it was a gas explosion, but if you want to claim insurance, you have to contact them." There was a pause. "Where have you been, Julie?"

"With a friend." It wasn't exactly a lie. Of course, with prompting, Colin could become more than a friend. "Mom, did you say *both* you and Dad had been worried about me?"

"Yes."

"Are you speaking to Dad?"

"Of course I'm speaking to your father," her mother answered. "This is a rather important event, Julie. Something's happened to one of our children."

"Did Eileen call you yesterday?"

"Your sister?"

Who else was called Eileen? But Julie didn't remark. "She told me she wants the china. Mom, don't give it to her."

There was a brief pause. "Julie, this is a strange time to discuss personal property. You weren't anywhere near that explosion, were you? Police checked with neighbors and some thought they saw you..."

"Mom, really, I'm okay. I'll tell you all about it soon. Right now I need you to phone the police and let them know I'm fine and will call soon."

Her mother sounded reluctant, but agreed.

Brad wasn't so easy to convince. She talked to her partner for about five minutes, assuring him that she was fine. A call interrupted them—one of his dates, she was sure—or she might still be talking. She was about to sit down, when she decided to phone Roger. First she called his home, and when there was no answer, she dialed the number of the resort in the Bahamas. Since he went there often she knew it by heart. While she didn't want to admit it, the things that Colin had mentioned about her partner were beginning to bother her, and she just wanted to prove to herself that he was there.

The operator took a while, but eventually she was connected. Roger answered and Julie laughed with relief. She didn't want to think her partner could be guilty of killing somebody. He might have flown in and out of town in a few hours, but things had been happening so quickly he couldn't possibly have returned to his yacht to receive her call to him now. Roger was equally jovial on the line, asking about the plant. She didn't mention her house or the body. She just told him she needed to know where some files were.

When she hung up she went to the booth where Colin sat waiting for her. He'd ordered tea for both of them.

"Everything all right?"

Julie nodded, sitting down. "I told Brad I'd be in to work Monday."

"Why did you do that?" Colin seemed angry at her. "You can't go to work. Julie, you can't go near the plant until I find out who the murderer or murderers are."

She stirred sugar into her tea. "Brad didn't believe me. It was the only way I could convince him that I was all right. I can call in sick if you really don't want me to go in. Did you order?"

"I didn't know what you wanted."

She glanced toward the front of the restaurant at the dessert bar. Julie had a bad habit. Whenever she was in turmoil she ate sweets. "Actually, I want a piece of cheesecake."

AFTER THEY'D EATEN, Colin got back on the expressway into the city. They had decided it was too late to stop and buy clothes. They would pick up something tomorrow. Besides, they were going to sleep. Since she doubted he would get her her own room, she didn't need much for the event. She could sleep in her clothes. She'd slept in her dress the night before and had survived. Now, at least, she had a hairbrush and a barrette. They'd fled the cabin too quickly for her to remember the canvas flight bag.

The city passed by, all brightly lit. Julie didn't pay much attention to where they were going until they got to a shabby neighborhood on the north side that kept getting shabbier the farther they drove. She had heard there were areas like this in Chicago, but she'd never seen them. The streets were dirty, littered with paper and garbage, the people not just poor, but destitute. The only bright spots were the taverns, one after another, stretching for several blocks. Neon signs flashed; honky-tonk music blared. Women in short leather skirts strolled seductively down the sidewalks. Since it was a summer night, other people congregated in corners or in front of the boarded-up storefronts, laughing and talking or playing craps.

Colin turned the car into an alley beside an old hotel and parked. The place was a dump, the cement blackened by years of soot and grime. A drunk lounged against some cans. The people passing by were either prostitutes or their clients, Julie couldn't tell which. "Are we going here for a reason?" she asked.

"Yes. This is where we're staying tonight."

"Here? You're registering for a room here?" Her shock was evident in her tone.

Colin frowned at her. "I told you we needed a good night's rest. Tomorrow's going to be a rough day. Aren't you tired?"

"This is a hotel for vagrants."

"Yes, it is." He kept frowning at her. "Is something wrong with that?"

"You're actually going to sleep here?"

He paused. "You know, Julie, for all we've been through, you don't strike me as the elitist type. Do you have something against hotels for vagrants?"

She wasn't the elitist type, and ordinarily she wouldn't have had a thing against them. Not that she'd choose to stay in one if she could go to the Ritz or even the Holiday Inn. But these hotels had bugs. And of all the things in the world Julie hated, it was bugs. She'd already told him that at the cabin. She reversed the question, "Do you have something against ordinary hotels?"

"Only that they're occupied by people who look and remember."

"You weren't concerned about being seen in the restaurant," she said. "We ate in a booth in a café in the middle of the northwest suburbs."

"We were there twenty-five minutes, during which I didn't close my eyes for a single moment. I want to sleep, Julie, not sit up and watch for a killer."

"I don't understand. Why here?"

"In case someone asks, no one will notice us here, and even if they do, they'll quickly forget. It's a way of life—see no evil, hear no evil, speak no evil. This is where people come to disappear, to drop out of society."

She frowned. She supposed he was right. She had hoped she would be thinking more like a detective by now. Why had she missed this logic? Growing stronger had appealed to her. Like this man appealed to her. She blushed at the sudden thought, and tried to ignore it. "It looks so sleazy," she said.

Colin followed her gaze. "It is."

"Isn't it dangerous?"

"Considering the options, it's the safest place I know."

She thought for a moment. "Won't someone hit us over the head and steal our money at a place like this?"

"I don't have much money on me. But yes," he finally admitted. "We'll have to be careful. It's a risk we'll have to take."

She nodded and climbed out of the car as Colin locked up. "Have you stayed here before?" she asked.

"I've been here before."

"I don't think I like your line of work."

He laughed. "You're the one courting danger, Julie. If I were you I would have run off a long time ago." He draped an arm around her and escorted her out of the alleyway, around the less savory characters.

"I tried," she said. "You wouldn't let me go."

She thought he'd laugh again, amused at her joke, but his expression was taut. "I wish I had," he said. "Now it's too late, and you need protection more than ever."

She was also scared more than ever. "Why more than ever? It was dangerous from the start."

"Because now you know too much."

"Too much?" Five little words. Five little chilling words. She frowned. "All I know is that we've been chased, nearly run over, my house has exploded—"

"Right," Colin said, as if that were the point. "The killer or killers—which is more likely, unless someone can be in three places at pretty well the same time to deposit a corpse in a refrigerator, explode a house and burglarize my home—are getting desperate. The longer you and I are free, the better our chances are of exposing them and the whole scheme, and they don't like that one bit."

"But, Colin, they're still trying to set you up. Why else plant the body in your cabin? What do they profit from killing you now? They wanted to blame you for that man's death." They were now in the busy lobby, talking in hushed voices as they waited to register behind several people.

"I don't know." He shrugged. "Maybe it's sheer panic. Maybe they're amateurs. That's something we'll have to find out." He didn't want to worry her, but the situation might be bleaker than either of them thought. Colin had a gut feeling that someone was shaping up a murder-suicide scenario, but the thought was too chilling to express. There was still much they didn't know.

Julie tried to ignore her surroundings as he signed the guest register and checked them in, paying cash. The clerk, slovenly and indifferent, barely glanced at them. A stooped, despondent man slumped beside the elevator. "We'll walk," Colin said, steering her around the assorted characters who peopled the lobby. "Check out the entrances and exits."

"I thought you felt safe here."

"I do, but I've learned to check out entrances and exits everywhere I go."

Julie walked with him up the steps. Paper and other debris littered the stairwell, and the carpet and walls were stained. She kept telling herself it wasn't so bad; it could be worse.

Despite her rationalizations, she almost ran the other way when he unlocked the door to their room and turned on the light. Several roaches scurried for cover. Only the colorful characters she'd seen below kept her fixed in the doorway. She might be tough, but she'd never make it on these streets alone.

"Not bad." Colin glanced around. He must not have seen the bugs. Shrugging off his jacket, he tossed it over a chair and went to the blinds to jerk them down.

Julie stared at the room. Aside from the double bed that was shoved up against one wall and sagged in the middle, the only other furniture was a straight-backed chair and a dresser with a mirror that had seen better times. The walls were as dirty as the ones in the hallway and the carpet was even more stained. The light was a single bulb, bare, set in a once-gold fixture, and the shades were a greasy shade of gray. The room was papered with red flocked birds.

"Want to get the door?" Colin said to her as he moved to turn on the lamp by the dresser. "Be sure and secure all the locks."

Julie wondered how long she would have stood there had he not spoken. Slowly she stepped inside the room and closed the door. The place might not have much in the way of amenities, but there were at least four locks on the door. "This is more secure than Fort Knox."

"People who come here don't like to be surprised."

She could well imagine. Besides Colin and her, the only people who would stay here were drug abusers, prostitutes and pimps. Maybe a mobster or two. How could she and Colin be safe? The killers themselves might be here. It seemed just the place.

Colin had taken off his shoulder holster and he started to unbutton his shirt. "Do you want to wash first?"

Julie hadn't noticed the metal pitcher of water sitting on the dresser next to a bowl. "Do you think they're clean?"

"It's water."

That didn't make the pitcher and bowl clean. She shivered, thinking of what could be in them. Germs. But he didn't seem to mind. "Go ahead," she said. "Is this the bathroom?" She pulled open a door. It was a mistake. Startled by the sudden light, more roaches scurried for cover.

"It's a closet," Colin told her. "The bathroom's down the hall."

Julie closed the door and leaned against it. "This is ridiculous. Colin, I can't stay here."

"Why not?"

"I can't stand bugs."

"They won't hurt you. They're afraid of you."

She shuddered. "You knew I hated bugs. I told you at the cabin. I'm not staying here," she said firmly.

"Julie, I'm tired. Could you please just bear it for now? I'll try to figure something out tomorrow."

"I can't sleep here. You can't expect me to sleep here."

Colin placed his hands on his hips, his feet spread wide in that aggressive stance of his that made her so angry. "Would you rather sleep somewhere the killer can find us?"

He was losing patience. She could tell by the tone of his voice. But Julie was upset, too. "I'm perfectly amenable to sleeping somewhere the killer can't find us," she answered. "I've told you before, I don't want to die. But I don't want to sleep with bugs, either."

"Aren't you making a big deal out of this?"

"To you, perhaps, it's a big deal. To me, it's perfectly logical. I can't stand bugs. And if you think that's a big deal, just watch." With that, she turned and started to unlock the door. "I'm leaving."

"Dammit, Julie," he said, striding to her and capturing her hands. "Will you please stop this nonsense? I'm tired and I'm not in the mood to fight with you."

"Then don't."

With the same defiance that had fueled her all her life spurring her into action, she reached for the lock again. This time Colin grabbed for her. Furious, she kicked at him, but he held her tight, trying to subdue her. They were face to face, body to body, her breasts crushed to his chest. Suddenly she became aware that she was thinking about making love with Colin. Whether she wanted to or not, she could feel every lean, hard inch of him. She stopped struggling and held her breath, waiting for him to say or do something to break the spell.

He stared down at her, vividly aware of the same thing. As angry as he was, all he could think about was the softness of her hips pressed against his thighs, her breasts brushing his chest with every breath she took. The feel of her skin, so silky, her hair, so fiery, as fiery as her temper. He wanted to bury himself in that softness, feel her next to him, naked. Lie beside her, in her. Trace his lips across hers. Who was he kidding? He hadn't just kidnapped her to protect her. He'd wanted to be with her.

"Julie?" he said softly.

"Yes?" Although she could have, she didn't move away. She kept leaning against him, full length.

"This isn't a very good idea."

"I know."

"I'm going to kiss you, anyway," he murmured huskily. "I've wanted to kiss you for a long time."

"I know."

Gently he brushed her hair back and cupped her face in his hands. For all the hardness of his body his hands were amazingly soft as they touched her. She'd noticed that before when he'd held her. She'd dreamed of his mouth. The softness.

But dreams didn't compare to reality. When Colin finally leaned his mouth down to hers and brushed her lips she felt a quiver in her stomach quite unlike anything she'd ever felt before, a soft fluttering that made her knees weak and her heart skip beats. His lips were soft and warm and wonderful, and she gave a little gasp of surrender.

Then suddenly there was no gentleness between them. He gathered her close and kissed her deeply. Passion surged through their veins like a heat storm on a summer night, made stronger because of the time it had waited on the horizon. His mouth tasted sweet. Her heart slammed against her rib cage as her breathing grew ragged. He slid his hands up and down her body, then cupped her breasts.

She felt on fire. Her nipples went rigid as he rubbed his thumb across them, lightly back and forth. She groaned with pleasure.

"God, Julie," he murmured against her lips. Then he pulled away. Abruptly. He strode angrily across the room. Frustrated, he raked a hand through his hair, his breathing ragged. "Damn," he swore. "I'm sorry, Julie. I didn't mean for that to happen."

Liar, his conscience nagged. *You meant every sweet caress. You wanted her completely, forever.*

He paced the room again, trying to regain control. The only thing that had stopped him was her response to him—her pressing against him, wanting him. A woman like Julie Hunter deserved more than he could give her, and she darn sure deserved more than a quick tryst in a flea-bitten hotel room.

Julie had just as hard a time getting her emotions in check. She felt stunned by the intensity of the embrace, weak and wrung out, and at the same time angry. Furious with the both of them. How could he just push her away like that? Excite her that way, then shove her aside? She was ashamed of the way she'd returned his passion, and she burned with anger.

"Neither did I," she said at last, pushing away from the door, where she'd had to lean to hold herself up. "I guess we'd both better get some sleep."

"I guess," Colin answered. "Do you want me to turn off the light?"

"No."

"You can have the bed."

"Thanks, but you go ahead. I'll sleep sitting on the chair."

"You'll be uncomfortable."

"That's nothing new." Right at the moment she was terribly uncomfortable. And embarrassed. Needing something to calm herself, she walked over to the bowl of water sitting on the dresser. She stared at it for a moment, then plunged her hands into it, splashing water on her face. Considering the danger she'd just put herself in, letting him kiss her—no, *wanting* him to kiss her—she may as well take her chances with a few germs.

Chapter Eight

She had a hard time sleeping. The chair was so uncomfortable she could hardly bear to sit, let alone close her eyes. She shifted and leaned her head against the dresser, trying to rest. It was close to four in the morning and still the neon sign outside the hotel window flashed on and off, bathing the room in red and blue hues even through the window shade. She could hear music blaring, the revelry of the streets, people coming and going. Down the hall doors opened and closed. Bedsprings creaked in the next room. Footsteps led up and down the stairs. She was exhausted just thinking about everything that was going on around them.

Colin snored away on the bed, seemingly undisturbed by the uproar. Julie actually considered joining him at one point, after squirming on the hard surface for the upteenth time. The only thing that kept her glued to the chair was the thought of what or who might have slept in the bed before him, and the fact that if she were to fall asleep beside him, she might very well wake up in his arms. Or worse, beneath him, making love with him. The memory of his kiss still lingered on her lips, burning through her like wildfire. The feel of his hands on her breasts, his body against hers, had seared themselves on her consciousness.

She gave a heavy sigh, willing herself to sleep. Oh, why had she gone back to the parking lot that night?

THE SOUND of a creaking floor woke Julie. She opened her eyes and stared at the ceiling. It took a few moments to realize she was in bed—in bed in a hotel for vagrants. How had she gotten there? She couldn't remember a thing. Turning her head, she glanced around. At least there weren't any bugs that she could see, and in the pale light of morning the place looked cleaner than she had imagined it last night. The sheets smelled of bleach and, the slightly musky scent of a man's shaving lotion lingered—Colin.

He stood at the dresser with his back to her, pulling on his shoulder holster and tucking his guns in place. His hair was wet, and although he hadn't shaved, it was obvious he had washed. He looked as good now as he had last night, perhaps more so, rested and refreshed. Julie sat up and pushed her hair back, running her fingers through the fiery locks. She looked awful in the morning.

As though sensing she was awake, he turned around. "Good morning. How are you feeling?"

"Awful."

"Did you get any sleep? You looked awfully uncomfortable leaning against the dresser."

She ran a hand through her hair again. God, she was tired. "How did I get into the bed?"

"I moved you when I woke up. Why do you keep fussing with your hair? It looks nice. You have lovely hair, Julie, so nice and long."

What was that supposed to mean? She glanced at him, trying to figure out what he was pulling. "You can compliment my hair all day, Colin. I still won't like this place."

He laughed. "You did okay."

"Sure, I slept in a chair most of the night."

As he gazed at her his expression sobered, and he said seriously, "You slept in a chair because of what happened between you and me, Julie, not because of any bugs."

She flushed. She felt uncomfortable talking about what had happened between them. She almost wished he'd left the subject closed. "I don't think we should discuss that, Colin. I'd like to pretend it didn't happen."

"So would I. But it did happen, and it's pretty hard to ignore." As he spoke he kept his eyes on her, studying her. Julie felt lost in his blue gaze. Tension grew between them, a flash of summer heat. She wanted to ask him if the embrace had meant anything to him, if he'd felt anything except passion, but he turned away. "Do you want to wash up? I got some fresh water from the bathroom down the hall."

She wanted to *go* to the bathroom. She tossed the covers aside and stood. "You left me alone in here?"

"I locked the door. Would you rather wash in the bathroom? I'll walk you there."

"Please," she said grudgingly. How could he just turn his emotions on and off so quickly? She slipped her gym shoes on and grabbed her hairbrush. Since she was already fully dressed she didn't have to do much more than straighten the wrinkles. Her ankle still hurt slightly and she flexed her foot. "Can I go by myself?"

He shook his head. "I don't think it's wise."

Probably not, not if the activity she'd seen and heard last night was any indication of what went on here. Someone could be lying in wait to kill her, just for her barrette.

"I guess I'm ready." She followed him out the door.

"We've got a few things to do this morning," he said as they walked down the hall. "As soon as you're finished we'll catch some breakfast and call Paul."

"Fine." Julie wasn't up to making plans. All she could think of was brushing her teeth and creating some semblance of order out of her hair. Her scalp tingled, as though little creepy things had crawled in it all night, and her mouth tasted like a sewer.

Colin paused by the bathroom door. "Take your time." He gestured to the telephone on the opposite wall a few yards away. "I've been meaning to check the calls on my answering machine. I'll wait over there for you."

She nodded. "Okay."

Then alone she faced a stained porcelain shower room that had seen better days.

COLIN WATCHED the bathroom door as well as all the other doors along the corridor as he spoke into the phone. Paul had answered right away. "Sorry," his ex-partner whispered into the phone. "The prints weren't good enough for an identification. I couldn't even get a partial."

"Okay, thanks. Anything on the car or flight plan?"

"Nothing on the car. The boys at the office are working on it as best they can. It's Sunday, remember. But there's something here on the flight plan you suspected might have been filed at O'Hare for small crafts." Colin could hear papers shuffle in the background. "As you guessed, Roger Perry flew in from the Bahamas around noontime, and left the same day around 10:00 p.m. He must have spent the day in Chicago."

Colin fell silent. Should he tell Julie, who would be stunned and upset? He decided to wait on that. It might mean nothing. "Anything else?"

Paul lowered his voice even more. "I hear a stiff came in from Wisconsin late last night. The Captain didn't want to say anything when I dropped by the office very early this morning. I wanted to check up on the things you asked for, but told the guys on duty I was there to pick up some weekend paperwork. I think it's the one they found in your cabin. It's at the county morgue."

"And?" Colin had always expected the authorities to bring the corpse to Chicago. First, there was probably a missing persons report filed with several surrounding states, and second, in the event of foul play, a corpse was automatically brought into the Cook County Coroner's Office. They could perform tests other coroners only dreamed of. "Was an autopsy done on him?"

"Later this morning."

"And an ID?"

"I would assume."

"Do you have it?"

"No. And I can't get it, either. The Captain's got it in his office. All I have is a case number—4610. And though no one has said there's a connection—an APB is out on you. I suspect they found a copy of your deed *very* quickly."

Damn, Colin swore to himself. The police were finally catching up; everything was coming to a head. If only he had some kind of lead as to what the heck was going on. It had been two days since the murder and he had barely gathered a single clue. He jotted down the number Paul had quoted.

"You ever been to the morgue?" his ex-partner asked.

"What?" Colin pulled his attention back to the phone. He'd been to the morgue thousands of times—with Paul. "Why?"

"They keep records there, you know."

Colin paused. "Yes, I remember. Going to meet me there?"

"Sorry, buddy. It's Sunday, my day at home. You're on your own. But if they want a cop source, just mention my name. If they call the department, they'll find out I was in first thing and left for the day."

"I owe you one, Paul."

His ex-partner laughed. "Bring your girl to dinner."

Julie. Colin glanced at the bathroom door as he hung up the phone and dug in his pocket for more change. It sounded funny to think of her as his "girl." At the same time, it sounded right. Leaning against the wall and watching for her, he dropped a quarter in the slot and dialed the number to listen to the calls on his answering machine.

WHEN JULIE EMERGED from the bathroom, Colin was still on the phone. Not wanting to be alone in the hotel room, she walked down the hall to stand beside him. "Anything?"

He shook his head, thinking how nice she smelled. Although she was still wearing jeans and a sweatshirt, her hair was damp where she'd combed it back, and she'd scrubbed her face until it had pinkened to a healthy glow. "Mostly calls from Gayle. She's having a hard time with Brutus. The cat's chasing him all over the place and he won't let anyone out of the house."

"What are you going to do?"

"Nothing." He hung up and took her elbow. "Come on, let's get some breakfast. Do you need anything from the room?"

"No." Everything she owned was on her back or in her hand. But she was confused by his brusque manner. "Did you call your friend at the police department?"

"Yes, but at his home."

"And?"

"And the prints weren't any good."

"So what does that mean?"

They had walked down the steps. Few people were up and about this hour in the morning—a couple of drunks slept on the sofa; a maid pushed her cart across the lobby. Another clerk was on duty. In the distance Julie could hear church bells, an odd juxtaposition.

"It means we're in trouble," Colin answered as they went out the door. "The body's at the county morgue, though. As soon as we eat breakfast I'll drop you off back here. I'm going to go see what I can find. If you don't hear from me in a couple of hours contact the police."

Julie knew without asking that the police had found the body and that they had connected the murder to Colin. She also knew she wasn't staying in the hotel room alone. "How are you going to get into the morgue?"

"By hook or crook," he said. "I don't really know. I'm going to have to play it by ear."

"Won't the police be looking for you?"

"They have an APB out on me. They discovered who owns the cabin, but the morgue isn't exactly on their list of places to check out in Chicago. I'll just have to be careful." They were nearly at the car. He glanced at her. "How did you know the police were after me?"

"After all we've been through, it didn't take a stroke of genius." She opened the door to her side and got in. "You can forget about dropping me off back here. I'm going with you."

"Where?"

"The morgue and wherever else you go. I'm not staying in that hotel room alone."

"Julie—"

"You can save your breath," she cut in. "I'm going."

They argued all through breakfast and during the ride to the county morgue. Julie was adamant. Risk or no risk, she wasn't about to sit around the sleazy dive and wait for him to come back. Colin finally sighed and turned onto Harrison Street. "If you're going to insist on doing this, please keep your mouth shut and don't mess up."

"I haven't done anything wrong so far, have I?"

His sidelong glare told her he didn't quite agree. She'd done everything wrong.

"Just don't say anything," he went on. "I'm going to have to bluff my way through this."

The county morgue was located in the basement of Cook County Hospital, one of the largest medical institutions in the world. Low estimates were that at least one hundred thousand people passed through the doors of the hospital annually. Principally a hospital for indigent patients, the emergency room alone was packed twenty-four hours a day. The only thing Julie remembered about the place was the burn unit, where rich and poor alike were helicoptered in.

Colin pulled into a parking space at least five blocks from the main building. "Why so far away?" she asked, thinking of the long walk back.

"This place is always busy. Cops are constantly around. I don't want anyone to get a make on the car."

"What if we need to get away fast?"

"We run." He smiled at her as they got out of the car. "Don't worry, Julie. Everything will be fine. We'll go in the front entrance. The morgue's in the basement, so stay close. If an elevator is handy, we'll ride down. Otherwise we'll take the stairs."

Although she knew he was amused by her questions, as she listened to his plans Julie felt like a real live sleuth. Is this how it was all the time solving criminal cases? Somehow she doubted there was as much tension. Just the thought of sneaking into the morgue gave her heart reason to palpitate. What if they got caught?

Colin was so familiar with the layout of the hospital he could have been an employee. They went in the front entrance along with hordes of other people and then down a side stairs. Just as many people were in the basement as upstairs. People in white, people in yellow, people in dress clothes and people in dirty clothes.

"Who are all these people?" Julie whispered to him.

"Doctors, nurses, patients, visitors, vagrants, you name it."

"Where are they going? This is a Sunday morning."

"Everywhere. This is Cook County Hospital. The place is as busy at ten in the morning on Sunday as it is at midnight on Monday." He turned down another hall. "Come on. This is it."

Julie's heart pounded with apprehension as they stepped forward. Anything could go wrong. Colin's thin smile reinforced her fear. "Let me handle the clerk," he murmured in low tones. "You pretend to be family of the dearly departed. All I have is a case number, so we're going to have to wing it and keep our fingers crossed. Just remember to look upset when you see the corpse."

That should be no problem. The past few times she'd seen the dead man, Julie had *been* upset!

Colin opened a door. Several people at desks inside the room looked up. The morgue itself was through a connecting door. Julie could see it as a clerk walked out and went to a file cabinet. A man going through a stack of papers continued to gaze. "May I help you?"

Colin flashed his detective badge. "We're here to view case number 4610. This is the family."

Julie was afraid they'd blown it when the man frowned and several minutes ticked by. "The family was just in."

"I know. We took them back to the station." Colin inclined his head at Julie. "This is a sister. I've been hired by the family on a related matter, and they wanted me to bring her in—"

"Does the department know you're down here?" the man asked. Colin nodded and gave the clerk Paul's name and badge number, prodding him to call the section Paul worked in. The man shook his head wearily, probably expecting a difficult day and not wanting to exhaust himself too soon. He reached into the drawer for keys. "That case is being transferred to the funeral home and we have an autopsy scheduled, so you'll have to hurry."

"We'll be just a minute," Colin said in that rumbling voice that inspired confidence.

He should be an actor, Julie thought as she watched Colin go through his routine.

The clerk walked ahead of them, and Julie couldn't bring herself to say anything. She kept thinking they were going to get caught at any moment; someone was going to realize they had no business there, and would report them to the police. Worse, she dreaded going into the large refrigerated room. As if sensing her fear, Colin took her hand. "It'll be okay," he murmured. "Chin up."

"I'm okay."

Soon they were standing in the cold sterile morgue before a wall lined with aluminum freezers. The clerk rolled one out, and Julie gave her obligatory peek, her distress very authentic. The clerk rolled the unit back in. Julie felt saddened, also glad that the dead man was at last going to rest in peace.

"That's fine, thanks," Colin said to the clerk as he locked up. "Do you think we could get a report?"

"I gave the last cop a report, and I can't get another without Mrs. Osgood's approval." He glanced at Julie and softened his harsh tone. "You understand."

Julie nodded. "Could you tell me how the police spelled my brother's name?" she said quickly to salvage the situation. "I want to make sure it's correct. It's often misspelled for some reason."

The clerk arched a brow, hesitating as if puzzled. Julie feared he would ask her how she thought it should be spelled, or refuse her completely. But instead, convinced at her grief, he turned around and went to a nearby table, where he leafed through some sheets. "*N-o-r-m-a-n O-s-g-o-o-d*," he spelled out clearly. "Says here he was a pawnbroker."

Julie shook her head vigorously, surprised to find the strength needed to carry out the ruse. "That's it. Sometimes people substitute a *w* for the *g*."

The clerk shrugged, dropped the papers back onto the now messy pile and led them back along the route they had come.

Out on the street Colin nearly lifted Julie in a bear hug. "You're a genius, Ms Hunter," he said.

"That's fine, but there are two men in blue over there, Colin, and we shouldn't draw any more attention to ourselves than necessary."

"Right," he agreed, and helped her into the car. But instead of rounding the car to the driver's seat, he strode casually over to the phone booth he'd spotted. Flipping through the phone book he found what he wanted and returned to the car.

"Well?" she asked as he pulled out into traffic.

"He's listed. The place is in the western suburbs."

BECAUSE IT WAS SUNDAY, the drive to the dead man's house took longer than it would have normally. Bells tolled for the faithful all over the city. Everywhere Julie looked people were dressed up for church. "I keep forgetting it's Sunday," she said.

"Everyone's busy." Colin glanced at her. "What does your family usually do on Sunday?"

By now Julie was accustomed to his penchant for unusual conversations in the midst of strife. The subject didn't seem a bit out of place, even though he didn't strike her as the philosophical type. "Visit, I guess, like everyone else."

"Does your family have big get-togethers?"

"Yes. My sister and brothers are all married and they all have children. We're always getting together for one reason or another, birthdays, anniversaries." Until her parents had filed for divorce. Then everything had come to an abrupt halt. No one wanted to do anything that would further inflame the situation. "What about your family?" she asked.

"Gayle usually has something going. My parents live out of state, so I don't see them all that often."

"Where do they live?"

"Georgia."

"You're from the South?" The more she knew about him the more she was surprised. That was something she would never have guessed.

"Born and raised." He affected a Southern drawl. "Ma'am."

She laughed. "When did you come to Chicago?"

"When I was a teenager and I got tired of farming onions." He turned off the busy street they were on, glancing at her as he drove.

She had a feeling that was something he didn't readily admit. Not that he was ashamed of it. He just seemed a private person.

"Ever seen onions grown?" he asked.

She shook her head. "No, I can't say that I have."

"They're a good crop. They just need a rich soil and a warm climate and a strong back at harvest time."

"You harvested by hand?" Another unexpected revelation. It must have been all that work that had made him so lithe and strong. Come to think of it, he looked like the type of man who had worked outdoors most of his life, doing strenuous physical labor. She'd thought him a football player.

"We didn't have a big farm, just enough to feed and clothe everyone."

"When did your sister come to Chicago?"

"Right after I did. She didn't care for farming, either."

"Anyone left to carry on the tradition?"

"No. My father finally sold most of the land to a housing development. He just raises a small crop now. Sits on his porch and watches the buildings go up."

"Do you like onions?"

He laughed. "The key question. I used to eat enough of them. We had onion everything."

What an odd combination. Farmer and private eye. "What brought you to law enforcement?"

"The hubcaps."

"Huh?"

"I went through a phase in my teens where I stole hubcaps. I grew out of it. Promise."

She wondered how many he had actually stolen. He had come to a stop sign, and she was still curious about his athletic background. Why not ask? "Colin, did you ever play football?"

"Yes, in high school. Why?"

"Just wondering. What was your position?"

"Running back," he said. "I carried the ball."

She couldn't be right all the time. They didn't talk much more. Colin had driven into an exclusive residential neighborhood. The area was old, with lush foliage and stately oak trees. The houses were all large and fancy looking, set well back on high fenced lots. Somehow she hadn't expected the man she had viewed in death to be wealthy.

"Keep an eye out," Colin told her. "In this neighborhood my car is like a neon sign. We could get reported."

"What do you want me to do?"

"Just be watchful. Look for cops.... Not bad," he remarked a few moments later as they drove by a particularly large home that sprawled for at least half an acre. The address matched the one in the phone book. A pawnbroker could afford this? In addition to the several late-model luxury cars in the circular drive, they could see a pool and a sauna to the side of the house.

Julie agreed. "He must be doing something right."

"Not anymore."

The finality of his statement brought her back to reality. Several people went in the house. Still others came out and drove away. Colin drove down the street and parked the car beneath a tree.

"Where do you suppose they're all going?" Julie asked.

Colin shrugged. "A family gathering to make arrangements for the funeral. Everybody's crying. Looks like they just found out. His wife was probably notified early this morning. She viewed the body, called friends and family, who then came to say they were sorry. Sometimes, when a person dies, more happens at the house than at the funeral."

Julie had forgotten that no matter what the man had done—if, in fact, he had done anything—someone somewhere had loved him and was sad that he was gone.

"We'll wait a bit until the family heads off to the funeral parlor, and the friends go home."

"And then what?"

"Then we need to take a look inside his house and see what we can find."

"What about security?" Julie couldn't imagine a house so large and fancy not having an alarm system. "We can't just walk in."

"There's probably an alarm system," he agreed. "Don't worry, I've circumvented them before. We'll have to be careful, but we'll get in."

They sat in the car, watching, for several long minutes. Julie thought the family would never leave. Finally all the cars pulled out of the drive, and the house settled into quiet.

"Ready?" Colin opened his door.

"Are you sure everyone's gone?" There could be maids, butlers. In this kind of neighborhood Julie assumed the homeowners would have servants.

"No, we'll just have to take a chance. I think his wife left with the last bunch."

Julie had also noticed the attractive older woman leaving. From the number of people that had come and gone, either the man had lots of friends and relatives, or he was a member of the Mob.

"I feel weird doing this," Julie murmured as they walked up the sidewalk to the driveway. "Why isn't the house sealed? The police should be here. He's a murder victim."

Colin shook his head. "There's no need to seal his house. He wasn't killed here. The police probably talked to his wife early this morning when they notified her. They'll return later to quiz her some more when things have settled down."

"We're not just going to go in the front door," Julie scoffed. She thought they should creep around the back and break in.

"We'll ring the doorbell for the benefit of the neighbors and servants, if there are any. Hopefully no one will be home. This is Sunday—even servants deserve a day off. Then I'll pick the lock and we'll go in. If anyone's watching, we'll look like bereaved relatives who have keys. It won't take but a minute."

What concerned Julie was that someone might answer when they rang the bell. Then what would they do? Pretend to be friends upset by the news? Surely the servants knew all the relatives. The house was silent, though, when Colin rang. They could hear the doorbell sound, cheerful melodic tones. He stood on the stoop like any other visitor, his hands tucked casually into his pants pockets, staring at the door. After a few moments, looking as cool as possible, he pulled some wires, fiddled with the door, and they were inside. Where had he learned all this? she wondered.

The house was even more opulent than she'd expected. Julie simply stood and stared at the chandelier and marble floor that graced the entrance. The jade vase alone that sat on a table had to have cost thousands of dollars. A huge oak staircase spiraled up to the second floor like something right out of a movie set. "My, God, it's gorgeous."

And she'd just lost everything.

Colin's low whistle echoed her sentiments. "Norman Osgood sure made some bucks in his lifetime. And not from a pawnshop."

"Doing what, then?" Julie asked.

"I think that's what we need to find out."

Colin bypassed most of the rooms with just a glance inside. Julie followed him in awe. Everything was stunning, one piece of antique furniture lovelier than the other. The house was stark white and black, marble and oak, silk and velvet. Finally Colin paused by what was obviously a study. A fireplace dominated the room, surrounded by a sofa and several chairs. Bookshelves lined another wall. A large mahogany desk stood in the corner by a window. "Let's start here."

Closing the door behind them, he went directly to the desk and started going through the drawers. Julie hung back. She felt like a voyeur. Somehow it wasn't right to invade someone's home, his privacy, even when your life was at stake. "Colin, I don't think this is a good idea."

"Why not?"

"It's the same as leaving Osgood in your cabin. Something about it seems... wrong."

He didn't even look up at her, just kept rifling through the desk. "I don't know about you, Julie, but

I don't relish going to jail for murder. If you don't want to help, that's fine. I understand. Just keep an eye out for the family coming home."

Julie still felt guilty. She stood by the door and watched Colin search the desk. He pulled out a ledger and leafed through it. Then he tossed it back inside. "Shouldn't you be more careful?"

"Why?"

"You don't want them to know we were here."

"The desk is a mess. There are a million papers in here. You'd think a guy this wealthy would have some kind of filing system or bookkeeping method."

"Did you find anything important?"

He shook his head. "Nothing that makes sense to me."

The doorbell rang. The lilting chimes echoed through the house, but to Julie, they sounded more like a fire alarm. She was already nervous. She jumped, glancing around as though she could see through the study door to the front entrance. "Who's that?"

"Just relax," Colin told her. "There's no one home."

"But what if it's the police?" she asked, her voice a whisper. "Are you sure you turned off the alarm?"

"Yes, I'm sure. It's probably friends, here to express their condolences."

Somehow that didn't allay her anxieties. Why had they come now, when the family was gone? Didn't they know the family was at the mortuary, making arrangements for the funeral? "What if they come in?"

Colin still didn't give her his full attention. He just looked up from his task for a brief moment. "Why would they ring the bell if they were going to come in?"

Julie wanted to point out that she and Colin had rung the bell, too, but she didn't say anything. She kept glancing at the door, thinking that any moment someone would burst through. If it was the police they would be dead. Except for the one entrance, there was no way out of the room.

Colin wasn't at all nervous. He kept searching the desk. He picked up an envelope and read the address. "Well, at least he files his income tax quarterly. That says something for him."

"Big deal," Julie said. "So do I. Along with about seventy thousand other people."

Colin actually smiled. "The government's got quite a racket going, making everybody pay his income tax on time."

Julie wrinkled her nose at him. "You wouldn't be so nice about it if you were one of the ones who had to pay."

"I do have to pay."

"Have you ever been charged a penalty? You get charged a penalty if you don't estimate right."

He laughed again and tossed aside the envelope. "Weird. A pawnbroker." He frowned as he studied the lavish surroundings. "You'd think that wouldn't account for this wealth."

Julie shrugged. "I guess that depends on how much he bought and what he sold."

"And what racket he was into," Colin said. He closed the drawer and grabbed her hand. "I'm afraid we're back to your company records. There's nothing here to tie Mr. Osgood to Lustre, Inc.—at least not his desk. But maybe there's something at Lustre that points to our prosperous pawnbroker friend who met with ill luck. Come on, let's go. Let's get out before somebody comes home and catches us."

Chapter Nine

Colin led Julie through the house so fast the place could have been on fire. He was about to jerk open the front door, when he came to a skidding halt. Because she was walking so quickly, she ran into him. "Damn!" he swore.

"What's the matter?"

Two narrow windows ran the length of the front door, one on either side. They were covered with very expensive lace curtains in a dotted Swiss pattern. Yet the intricate design didn't block the view of the two policemen who stood on the stoop. When one of them leaned to press the doorbell, Colin scowled. "That's what's the matter. What are the cops doing here? I know it's not the alarm. It's inoperable. Maybe somebody reported my car."

"Maybe they plan to question Mrs. Osgood again?" Julie suggested.

Colin glanced around, looking for a way out, as the chimes lilted through the house. "Maybe. But we can't hang around here." He took her hand again. "Come on, let's go out the back way."

Julie followed him through the house, all the while hoping the two officers would leave. Colin had parked down the block on purpose, and to reach the car, they'd have to cross open ground. Even assuming they made it to the car in one piece, she dreaded what would follow. She felt as though all she'd done for the past two days was ride around in his beat-up automobile—or run to it. She wasn't up to another chase. They'd had to drive like maniacs several times now, and each time she got a few more gray hairs.

They went out the kitchen door. Colin pulled her along, staying in the shadows of the house. They skirted the side, stepping in the flower beds and crushing the marigolds. The flowers sprang back slowly, one at a time. Julie could see the pool. Up close it was lovely, blue and serene and sparkling. The surrounding trees spread dappled shade over the water. Here and there a leaf floated, looking out of place on the ultraclean surface.

"Are they still there?" she asked when Colin paused at the corner of the house and glanced around to the front. She didn't see a police car, but it could be in the driveway.

"I don't know—" he sounded disgusted "—there's a bush in the way."

Since this was a cul-de-sac, they had no choice but to cross the lawn, directly in the policemen's view.

"Why don't we just talk to them?" Julie asked.

"And say what?" From the tone of his voice Julie could tell he didn't think that was a great idea.

"Good morning?" She could be facetious, too. She glanced at the pool again. It looked so cool and inviting on a hot day. A large, open bottle of chlorine sat by the pump, as though someone had been about to add the chemical, but had been called away. Probably to hear about his loved one.

"Colin," she whispered, coming up with an idea, "maybe we could pretend to be part of the pool-cleaning crew."

Turning his head, he looked at her. Then he flicked his gaze to the pool. "And do what?"

The question irritated her as much as it had him. "Leave. Get away."

"Pool cleaners have trucks," he said. "And uniforms."

"Do the police know that? They're thinking about the dead man. By the time they figure it out, we could be in the car and gone. We could carry the chlorine and pool equipment."

He glanced from her to the pool again and back. "Are you up to a run?"

"If you carry the chlorine."

"What if they're gone?"

What could she say? "Then I guess that along with everything else, you'll be guilty of stealing."

He stared at her for a long moment. "This is serious, Julie."

She was being serious. She felt ridiculous crouching beside a house and trying to peek through a bush to see if the police were in the driveway. "Well, what if they're gone? We're standing here arguing."

"All right. Good point. Let's go. I'll get the chlorine."

For all her bluster, Julie wasn't at all certain her plan would work. Or if the police would be there. As though tired of the hiding game, too, Colin walked straight across the yard to the pool, picked up the chemical and started for the front gate. Not knowing what else to do, Julie grabbed the leaf skimmer and followed him. She got as far as the edge of the house and stopped. Just before she stepped into the open she took a deep breath and closed her eyes.

It was almost with a sense of disappointment that she looked over to the front stoop and saw that the police were gone. She and Colin must have argued so long, they were unaware when the men left. "Colin, they're not here."

"Great. Let's go. The neighbors could be watching."

Julie tossed aside the skimmer and followed Colin to the car. He set the chlorine down and turned to her, spotting her disappointment. "Julie, do you want me to make the police come back so you can stroll across a lawn with a leaf catcher in your hand?"

"No."

"Then why are you wearing such a forlorn face? The police left. That's what we wanted them to do."

"I don't know..." she said, as puzzled as he was. "I was so prepared. I wanted to know if it would work."

He simply stared at her. "Sometimes you don't make sense. Let's get out of here."

Julie slammed her car door as Colin opened the trunk and placed the chlorine inside. When he slid onto his side she was still angry, though she couldn't for the life of her explain why. They'd gotten away without a high speed chase, too. Disappointing.

"Why did you take the chlorine?" she asked.

"I don't know. Just to steal something, I guess."

That didn't make sense, either. But, then, what had in this crazy puzzle? "Where are we going?"

"Back to the hotel. We still need to talk."

She sighed. "You should host a talk show."

"What are you upset about, Julie?"

"I don't know." She knew she was carrying on ridiculously. She just couldn't help it. She was so tired of running and being frightened. She crossed her arms defiantly over her chest. "What do you want to talk about?"

"Lustre, Inc."

"What do you want to know?"

"All kinds of things. How you process out the silver, who's involved, where they live, what they do in their leisure time, what your partners are like—"

"That would take a year," she cut in. "Maybe we should go to the plant, instead."

He glanced at her again. "Are you trying to play private investigator now?"

"No, I'm just tired of being chased and doing stupid things to avoid someone who isn't there. Can't we go to the plant? I thought you wanted to check the records or something."

"It's too early to go there," he said. "We have to sneak in. If there is a connection, and someone at Lustre knows about it, I don't want to alert them. I want to wait until night."

"George will be there."

"I'm sure we can get around one old man. He wasn't too much of a threat Friday night."

"What do you plan to do, hit him over the head?"

"No, I plan to sneak in without his seeing me. Do you have a security system in addition to a guard?" he asked, turning back on the highway that led to their ramshackle hotel.

"The doors are on sensors after we leave."

"Good. I can take care of them easily."

The way he talked, Julie wondered why they'd spent thousands of dollars installing the system.

"We still need some clothes," he went on. "Feel like stopping at a department store?"

That was about the best thing he'd suggested all day, Julie thought. That and lunch. After they went shopping they stopped at a small hot-dog stand on the next block. Several families had stopped, too, parents and children. The kids ate sticky Popsicles that dripped down their hands and legs, while their parents sipped sodas. Since it was such a nice day out, Colin led Julie to an area set up with umbrellas and lawn chairs.

"I'm sorry," she said when they sat down. She had simmered and stewed ever since they'd left the Osgood house.

"For what?" Although his expression was serious, she could tell he was amused. His eyes were alight with humor.

"For being cranky."

He couldn't contain his laughter anymore. He started to chuckle. "Tell me, Julie, are you Irish?"

"Yes."

"I thought so, with that red hair."

All her life she'd hated aspersions cast on her hair and all her life she'd put up with them. "Remarks about either my ethnic background or my hair will get you an even crankier disposition."

"Sorry. No offense meant."

She shrugged. "That's okay." She'd started out apologizing. She didn't want to argue with him again. Funny how things changed. Before she'd been helping him because she was involved and had no choice. Now she was helping him because she was concerned about him.

"Look," he said, placing his hands on her arm. "I know how you feel, Julie. I feel that way, too. This is frustrating, running and hiding and not getting anywhere."

Except getting more and more enamored of him. The entire time they'd been together she'd tried to ignore the attraction she felt whenever she was near him. As he sat in the chair, the wind ruffling his hair and the afternoon sun warming his skin, his hand rested gently on her arm, as if it belonged there. Sometimes the whole situation seemed so unreal to her. They were sitting here in the open on a bright sunny day, eating hot dogs and discussing their plight the way some people talked about getting their toddlers into nursery school. And her plight was more than finding a murderer. "I guess I'm tired."

"We've done some running. When we go back to the hotel we can both get some rest before we go to the plant tonight. You know, for the first time I feel good about this case. I'm certain Lustre is involved in some way."

Julie winced. "You think my partners—Brad and Roger—are involved. Do you know that when you suspect them, you're suspecting my ability to judge character? After all, I picked them to work with."

Colin pressed his lips together, gathering the strength to reveal what he'd learned. "Julie, in my last conversation with Paul, this morning, he told me that Roger had filed a flight plan at O'Hare with a ten o'clock departure time. He is also listed as having arrived in a small Cessna around noon on Friday. He was in Chicago the day of the murder."

Julie stared at Colin a moment. This was it; the big private investigator was tying together all the loose ends. It was circumstantial evidence, but it all seemed to conveniently point in one direction. Her ire returned full force. How dared he? "That means nothing, Colin, and you know it. He may have come in to pick up supplies, or some of those much touted sausages we've talked about."

Colin sighed. He should have known she would react like this. In some ways he felt relieved; he could deal with her anger, but not her despondency and hurt. "I'm sorry Julie. I don't know. I'm just giving you the facts as they were revealed to me. Suppose, just suppose, you don't know everything about your partners."

"I know they wouldn't cheat, murder, or set up Colin Marshall. That's all I need to know. And I know that Lustre employs about fifty people and it could be any one of them."

Colin looked sorry. She could be right. He brushed aside a strand of her hair that had fallen across her cheekbone. He wished he didn't care about this woman; it would make things easier. "Okay, Julie, you may be right. It doesn't necessarily have to be Roger and Brad. It could be someone else. All we should do now is search for some sign that Lustre worked with Norman Osgood."

"That's fine," she said, inching away.

"Something wrong?" he asked.

"No." She just didn't want to be touched by him, to feel all amiss and vulnerable. She picked up her hot dog and rearranged the onions. "Do you think these could be from your farm?"

"It's not likely."

To Julie, nothing was likely, particularly her attraction to him. What was she going to do? She didn't need a man in her life. She didn't want to be hurt again. Yet along with running from a murderer, she seemed to be barreling toward something that was even more frightening.

IN THE BRIGHT SUNSHINE Julie thought the neighborhood they entered looked much the same as it had last night and this morning, only the neon lights were missing. Even the taverns were open and it was just early afternoon. Colin parked the car and they walked to the hotel. Although the lobby was beginning to get busy, no one glanced their way as they trekked up the steps to their room. She hadn't realized how tired she was feeling. She'd almost fallen asleep in the car, and when he opened the door the bed actually looked inviting.

Colin placed the packages from their earlier shopping spree on the dresser. There was soda, toothpaste, candy bars and bug-spray. As though reading her mind, he said, "Don't get comfortable, Julie. We still need to have that talk."

She sat on the bed. "I think I can probably stay awake for about ten minutes."

"In a sitting position?"

"We can't talk with me lying down?"

That was a mistake and she knew it. But Colin ignored her unintended innuendo. "You'll go to sleep. By the way, what about the bugs? Aren't you afraid of them anymore?"

Julie was so tired she was beyond fear. Except where he was concerned. Being in a hotel room with him—any hotel room—was dangerous. "I think you were right, Colin. They're afraid of me."

He seemed surprised. "Well, she admits I was right."

Sometimes he took too much latitude. "You don't have to be nasty, you know."

"Okay, Julie, seriously, I need some information."

Drawn by his tone, she glanced at him. He was serious. He opened a soda and handed it to her. Then he took one for himself and sat in the chair across from her.

"What do you want to talk about?" she said.

"Silver. How it's recovered. We know Norman Osgood had silver under his fingernails. We know Lustre's parking lot was chosen for a setup. The more I understand about the recovery process, the better. So how's it done?"

That was a difficult question. Julie sighed as she thought about all the intricacies of recovering silver. "It's really complicated, Colin. I don't even know how to start. I guess it really depends on which method you use," she went on. "There are several, all the way from chemical to thermal to a new process that employs enzymes. These little germs eat away the waste material. Which one do you want to know about?"

"If we're going to solve a murder, I suppose how your company recovers it."

That did seem logical. "We use a chemical method, but it's employed two ways, depending on what we're processing. If we're doing film baths, we use a tank we buy from a supplier. Most of the silver has dropped off the film already, and is in the solution. We just have to combine it with a compound and recover it. With scrap film and paper, we have to use a different process. Still chemical, though."

"What's scrap film and paper?"

"Solid waste. Old film, again mostly X ray and photographic. In addition to the developing solutions, hospitals and manufacturing plants have solid waste. We buy it in bulk form and process it to stay competitive in the marketplace."

"And this business is lucrative?" he asked. "There's a real market for silver these days?"

Julie nodded. "Absolutely. Silver is used in so many things, jewelry, the film industry, dentistry, silverware. And that's just to name a few. There's even a quarter ounce of silver in every car that's manufactured today. The value fluctuates, of course, but there's always a market for it."

"Isn't silver mined? What about ore production?"

"The annual production of ore could never meet the demand for silver in today's marketplace. Just in the film industry alone, estimates are that the free world uses four hundred million troy ounces of silver annually. That's equivalent to thirteen thousand metric tons."

Colin whistled. "That is a lot."

She nodded. "There's never been anything found to equal silver as a light-sensitive material capable of forming a photographic image." She took a sip of soda, warming to her subject. She liked her business and she liked talking about it. Brad always told her she was their best sales tool. "It's amazing when you think about it," she went on. "In addition to regular old photographs, of which the American public takes millions monthly, there are hospitals, manufacturing plants as well as thousands of factories that use X rays."

Colin leaned back in the chair, studying her. Yet he was really thinking. He took a sip of his soda. "You mentioned you used another chemical process."

"Yes." She nodded. "We use cyanide. We're thinking of switching to an enzyme method—Virgil brought me the papers on it last Friday night—but for now, cyanide is the most efficient and cheapest method of chemical recovery in the industry today."

"Cyanide as in hydrocyanic acid?"

"Yes."

"The same thing that's used in gas chambers to kill people?"

She didn't like the judgment in his tone. "We don't combine it with sulfuric acid," she said, "and drip it into a roomful of people. But, yes, it's the same chemical. We're very cautious. There have been a couple of deaths in the industry due to cyanide poisoning, and everyone takes special precautions."

"How's it stored?"

"In lead-lined storage tanks."

"Is it ever just sitting out?"

"When we're in the midst of an actual recovery process it's just sitting out. Then it's in vats. We have to put the film in the chemical somehow. But normally the concentrated chemical is stored in tanks along the wall."

"How are the vats filled?"

"With a hose running from the storage tank. Colin, what does all this have to do with the murder?"

"Nothing, really. It just helps me to understand everything." He got up and opened another cola. He stood at the dresser drinking it with one hand tucked in the back pocket of his jeans. The day was hot and perspiration dampened his shirt. He turned back to her. "How do you hire your employees? Do you do any security checks?"

"Just the usual, credit checks and references. Sometimes we'll run a background check."

"Do you ever find discrepancies?"

"Colin, not many people are anxious to work in a factory that uses cyanide," she said. "They generally don't lie."

He smiled. "Point taken. How'd you get hooked up with Lustre? A young, attractive woman with two male partners."

She was taken about by his innuendo. "You make it sound sleazy."

"I don't mean to. I'm just curious."

"I was a management major at college. I interviewed, got the job and was offered a partnership a few years later when Roger and Brad wanted to expand."

"Why you?"

"I don't know. I guess because I was a good manager." She met his gaze, and returned it with a direct challenge. "What are you trying to say?"

"Nothing. What is it you do know about Roger?"

Julie was growing more and more irritated by the moment. She didn't like getting the third degree. "He's happily married."

"Anything else?"

"No. Look, Colin. Again, just because he was in town the day of the murder doesn't mean he committed it. That's why he bought that plane in the first place—so he could fly it. Why should he stay in the Bahamas for an entire three week vacation?"

"Julie, I'm not making any accusations."

"Then what's the point of all this?"

"I'm just trying to understand, trying to figure out a lead."

"Then why don't you let me call Roger in the Bahamas and ask him directly what he was doing in town?"

Colin set his cola down. "No, Julie. I don't want you tipping him off and causing a panic. If we can't find anything in the files, we'll go that route, but not yet. You have a lousy temper, Julie."

"I'm not even angry. You should get me angry."

He laughed. "Unfortunately, I have. Look, I'm sorry this is uncomfortable for you. Do you mind a few more questions? If you do, I'll shut up."

What was the difference? She shrugged again. "Fire away."

"When you joined the company as a partner, did you put in a lot of money?"

"No. Hardly any." She set down her soda. "You see, despite everything, I am good at my job." Although she'd assured him she didn't mind, Julie was tired of his questions. "Colin, isn't it more logical that the murderers are people connected to you rather than to me?"

He went back to the window and stared out. The sun fell on his face, and he took another swig of soda. "I think they're connected to us both, Julie. But who they are I don't know."

"How are we going to find them?"

He shrugged and left the window. "I'm hoping some of your personnel records will tell me the answer, or at least give me a lead. When I take a look at them tonight, I'll try to put some names together with some cases I've had that have gone sour, or with people who have a vendetta against me. You're right that Lustre employs dozens of people, who may be our murderer."

"Who would have a vendetta against you?"

"Julie, I'm a former cop. I've put a lot of people in jail."

"I noticed you used *I*." That was the second time he'd used the singular. "Are you going alone?"

He didn't answer for a long moment. "I'd like for you to stay here. It could be dangerous."

He didn't know the meaning of danger. Probably because he wasn't afraid. She shook her head. "You're not going to leave me alone in this hotel room."

He sighed. "I thought you weren't afraid. You made peace with the bugs."

"The bugs are the least of my concerns. These people may not look at you or talk about you to someone, but they sure wouldn't hesitate to stick a knife in your back. We not only have a killer after us and the police trying to catch up, we're surrounded by deadbeats and degenerates."

"I don't think it's quite that bad."

"Did you look at these people, Colin? Did you take a good look around this hotel?"

He'd been too busy looking at her. After last night when he'd kissed her, she was nearly all he'd thought about. He had to get over her, stop letting her affect his reasoning. "They aren't exactly the cream of the crop, but don't underestimate these people, Julie. They may be down on their luck, but they're human beings just like everyone else in this world."

She knew he was right. For all her complaining, she was the one who had been judgmental. "I'm sorry."

"No problem."

He might think the issue of her accompanying him was resolved, but she had every intention of being at his side that evening.

"Listen. It's five o'clock. We've got some time to kill. If you're not too tired we could get a shower. You can go first. I'll stand watch for you."

"Am I dirty again?"

He smiled. "No more than me."

Deep in her heart Julie knew it was a bad idea to take a shower in a sleazy hotel. Where was she going to go when he showered? She couldn't stand watch outside the door. She couldn't sit beside the tub, either. Yet she couldn't resist. At least her ankle felt better, and she no longer resembled the Hunchback of Notre Dame when she walked.

A half hour later, Julie came out of the shower, feeling fresh and scrubbed, her hair glistening. Colin winked at her as he stood by the door, letting her pass. He conducted her back to the room, let her in and, before departing, said, "Why don't you take a quick nap? I won't be back for a while. Lock the door behind me. I'll take the keys to let myself back in."

Julie shot him a fake smile. "Thanks. But if you think I'm returning for the evening while you run off, forget it."

He waved and flashed that white-toothed grin before disappearing behind the door. Julie locked it and found she wouldn't mind closing her eyes a moment. But before she did, she put on her jeans and sweatshirt, which she had draped over the desk chair. The mattress felt softer, less lumpy than the evening before, and before she knew it, she had drifted into a deep, profound sleep.

Julie knew the moment she awoke that Colin was gone. The room was dark except for the light on the dresser. It cast an eerie glow on the bag of food beside it, cold and greasy. How long had she slept? Why hadn't he wakened her? More important, where had he gone now?

Her thinking was still fuzzy. Everything was quiet—too quiet. She tossed back the covers and sat up, brushing her hair out of her eyes. She'd fallen asleep with it wet and it frizzed around her face in scraggly tendrils. She sat for a moment just thinking—and waiting. But nothing happened. No one came to the door, least of all him. After a moment she stood and went to the window, looking out, trying not to let panic grip her. It all came back in a flood. He'd gone to her plant. Without her.

Before she could change her mind, she grabbed the jacket Colin had bought her and opened the door to the hallway. A line stretched down the hall from the bathroom, tattooed men and leather-dressed women. Nighttime in the city.

She put her head down and hurried away.

Chapter Ten

Julie had run out of the hotel without a single clue as to how she was going to get to the plant. She stopped dead in her tracks on the sidewalk. She didn't have money, not a cent, and if Colin was gone he'd taken the car. She could hardly walk there. That would take her all night. What she needed was to reach her parents' home, and pick up some cash and the extra set of plant keys.

She glanced around, trying to think of a plan as a group of teenagers shoved by her. One of them smiled and leered. "Hey, red, ain't you a cutie? Wanna have a good time?"

She was in no mood to jolly a kid. She glared. "Shove it, kid."

He held up his hands in surrender. "Just asking, Momma. Can't blame me for asking. You're a looker."

"Right."

"You bet."

If this kept up, she'd be there all night.

She whirled around and started the other way down the street, ignoring the catcalls both behind and in front of her. A cab pulled to the curb. A woman got out and gave the driver a twenty.

Julie stood there for a full minute, staring. Why not?

Shouldering her way through the crowd of people going nowhere, she rushed over to the cab and poked her head through the open side window. "Can you take me out west?"

"California?"

Julie stared at him a moment. The last time she'd gotten a con man. Now she had a joker. "No, the northwest suburbs."

"Sure." He smiled broadly. "For double."

This one was a con man, too. They were all alike. Humanity. She didn't bother to bargain with him, just hopped into the cab. "It's a deal."

"Where to?"

Julie gave him her parents' address, hoping her mother would not only give her the keys to the plant, but loan her some money to pay the cab fare. If not, she was in trouble, this driver didn't seem overly friendly.

Yet once they got going he was exceptionally friendly, laughing and chatting. Although she didn't respond except for an occasional nod or a smile here and there, he gabbed on, telling her about everything, from his ailments to the kinds of passengers he transported. Sunday night traffic around O'Hare was beastly. She had forgotten about all the businessmen taking flights to meetings the following morning, and when they stalled, bumper to bumper, on the ramp leading to the airport and the driver droned on, she wanted to get out and walk.

"Could you step on it?" she said at last.

He glanced in the rearview mirror at her. "You in a hurry, lady?"

"Yes. Very much so."

"Why didn't you say so? If I get a ticket will you pay it?"

"Sure."

"And I get a ten-dollar tip."

"Yes, fine."

Telling him that was a mistake. In one quick spin of the steering wheel, he whipped from the line of traffic onto the shoulder of the road, barreling down it faster than she'd thought possible, faster than Colin had ever gone. Less than ten minutes later he screeched to a halt in front of her parents' house. Julie thought her heart was going to explode from beating so fast. She leaned back in the seat, shell-shocked.

"We're here."

"I know," she said, taking a deep breath to calm her trembling heart. "Thanks." She scooted from the seat. "Wait here I'll be right back."

He glanced at her with a surprised expression. "What about my money?"

"That's what I'm getting," she called over her shoulder, nearly running up the steps to the door. "We've got somewhere else to go."

"If it's out here, it's double," he shouted.

"Fine," she yelled back. "Just wait for me."

As usual the living room light was burning, a habit her mother had gotten into when Julie and her brothers and sister had all been teenagers and she'd leave a light on for them to come home to at night. They had joked about it being the eternal flame. All these years she still did the same. Mothers.

Colleen Hunter opened the door when Julie rang the bell, shock evident on her face. "Julie! Are you all right, dear?"

"I'm fine." She pushed her hair back, knowing she looked a mess and not at all all right. "Is Dad here?"

"He's asleep."

"Good." Julie could never fool her father. He always read her. "Mom, I know this is going to sound strange, but I haven't got time for explanations. I need my extra keys to the plant and I need some money. I have to pay a cab."

"You didn't call them as you promised, Julie. The police were here."

Julie frowned. "What did they want?"

"I don't know. They're still looking for you."

"Didn't you tell them I had contacted you and that I was all right?"

"Yes, but they really wanted to speak to you."

Julie nodded. "Okay, Mom, I will. Soon. But look, I need the keys and the money."

"The keys are no problem," Mrs. Hunter said. "I have them right here. How much money do you need?"

"How much do you have?" Julie countered.

The woman shrugged. "Fifty or sixty dollars, maybe. I might also have some grocery money."

"I'll take it."

"All?"

"Yes, please," Julie said. "I really have to hurry."

Her mother kept frowning. "Are you in trouble, Julie?"

"No, Mom. I'm fine. I am," she reiterated. "I'm just in an awfully big hurry."

Mrs. Hunter paused. "You remember when you were in high school and you asked me for money so you could go to the beauty shop?"

Julie had planned to bleach and straighten her hair. She'd changed her mind at the last minute and splurged on a new dress, instead. "Yes, why?"

"You said you were fine. I didn't believe you then, and I don't believe you now."

Julie smiled. "But you gave me the money."

"That's because I love you."

"I wasn't in trouble."

"That's true." Colleen Hunter laughed and went for her purse. She came back with several bills crumpled in her hand. "I won't bother to ask you any questions, Julie," she said, handing her the cash. Then she reached around the corner for the keys she kept hanging on the wall. "Just be good, and please be careful."

Julie could see now how parents helped their children. Even a murderer's parents. It was love. "I will. Thanks for trusting me, Mom." She clutched the items in her hand and started down the steps. Abruptly she turned back. "Mom, are you and Dad getting along any better?"

"Actually, your father and I are doing fine," her mother said with a smile. "I think we might even reconcile. I went down to the shopping center to inquire about a little job, and then I came home and broke the china."

"You what?" Julie was stunned.

"It was just cheap old stuff, anyhow," Colleen Hunter went on. "I wanted some new china, and I didn't want you children arguing over it, so I broke it."

She had broken more than china. She'd broken tradition. Julie rushed back to hug her mother. After forty years Colleen Hunter was finally becoming assertive. "I love you, Mom."

"I wish I knew what you were up to, Julie."

"If I could tell anyone, Mom, it would be you." Julie waved and hurried away. At the last minute she turned back and blew her mother a kiss.

The cabbie had grown impatient by the time she hopped back in, but Julie peeled off a hundred dollars and asked him to hurry to the plant. She'd spent so much time getting there that if she didn't move quickly, Colin would be gone by the time she arrived. If, in fact, he was still around.

When they pulled up near the industrial area she was even more aware of the darkness surrounding the plant. The night sky was black, with few stars, no moon. Only the streetlights on the cross street illuminated the area. She looked around for Colin's car, but she couldn't see the old beater anywhere. Perhaps he was already gone. Then again, he wouldn't park in the open where he could be seen. She'd have to go in the plant to find him. Or at least near it.

"Pull up over there," she said to the cabbie, gesturing to the cross street. She'd have to sneak in herself. She didn't want to alert George to her presence, and in turn alert him to Colin's presence.

"By the car?"

"Yes." How ironic. While Colin's car wasn't around, her red Mustang sat in the same spot she'd left it Friday night. She opened the cab door. "Thanks a lot."

"Thank you, lady. Look out for the dark. It's pretty desolate out here."

"Yes," she agreed. If she ever got out of this mess and went back to work, she was going to insist they spend money installing lights, no matter what the cost.

She crept across the parking lot much the same way she had the night she'd found the body, hugging the buildings and staying in the shadows. But she didn't have a purse this time to use as a shield. Just being at the plant, her heart had already started to thud with anxiety. She kept looking around, feeling more apprehensive by the minute. Anyone could come popping out of the trees at her. The killer. What if the murderer was waiting for them to come back?

By the time she reached the building itself, Julie was breathless from tension. She could see George by the window, talking on the phone as always, the newspaper spread out before him. In fact, everything seemed normal. She knew it wasn't.

Still determined to see if Colin was there, she slipped around to the back. If nothing else, maybe she could steal the files he wanted and take them back to the hotel. She'd get some invoices, too. Something that showed a connection to Norman Osgood, pawnbroker and millionaire extraordinaire. She'd take the stuff back and they could go over it later—if Colin was still alive. It occurred to her that the murderer might have killed him. He could be lying in the grass dead, a bullet in his chest, blood soaking the ground. She glanced toward the trees, at the leaves rustled by the wind.

Stop it, Julie, she commanded. She was letting her imagination get her again. Nothing was wrong with Colin. He was fine! She was the one in trouble. If she wasn't careful she was going to get caught.

When they had installed the alarm system, they had designed it so that anyone going into the plant with a key was automatically bypassed. She could see the new wood where the doorjamb had been replaced. The locks were fine. She inserted her key and crept inside. The moment she closed the door she had to pause and wait for her eyes to adjust to the darkness. With cyanide, it was too dangerous to move around and perhaps trip, knocking a hose off the wall or falling over a vat. That would be one quick way to end her life. Once she could see slightly, she started toward the offices.

The plant was laid out so that the offices were separated from the work area by a door. And then those offices were separated from the front office-reception area by another door. If she didn't make any noise George wouldn't hear her at all. She could even turn on the light and it wouldn't alert him. *If she didn't make any noise.*

Colin was nowhere to be found, and if the files were an indication, he hadn't been there at all. They remained unruffled. Julie made it to Brad's office first. She took a few files from his drawer, all the shipping invoices, and then crept to her office, looking for personnel files. Because the cabinet was in the corner, she switched on the lamp by her desk. It cast a soft glow over the room. Carefully, listening for any noise, she slid open a drawer. Everything was there that she could see. Not knowing what Colin could use, she grabbed the whole batch of files and placed them under her arm. The only thing she could do was go back to the hotel and wait for him.

She'd clicked off the lamp and started to turn around, when someone grabbed her from behind, slipping one hand around her waist and the other over her mouth.

Terror gripped her, but she didn't relinquish her hold on the files. Oh, God, after all this someone was going to kill her. She could tell it was a man.

"Don't make a sound," an angry voice whispered in her ear. "I swear I'm going to—"

"Colin," she breathed, trying to turn around. "Oh, Colin, thank goodness it's you."

He whirled her into an embrace.

"You'd better thank someone. What the blazes are you doing here, Julie? Why on earth did you leave the hotel?" The questions were rapid-fire, one after the other, angry and unrelenting. His body felt good against hers, lean and hard like his tone. She knew he was frightened. "What are you trying to pull?"

"I thought you were gone," she murmured when he took his hand off her mouth. "I woke up and you weren't there."

"So you decided to come down to the plant and play cat woman and break in. You could have gotten killed. Darn, you could still get killed."

"I thought you came here," she explained. "I thought you left without me. I just wanted to help."

"I was in the bathroom, shaving! Why _didn't_ you look for me?"

She noticed his chin didn't catch her hair. She also noticed he roiled with anger. "Why didn't you leave me a note? I had no idea where you were."

He glared at her, furious, more furious than she'd ever seen him. "What did you want me to write it with? Soda pop on the mirror?"

"Colin, I'm sorry. I didn't mean to—"

"Shh!" He clamped his hand over her mouth again and glanced toward the door, as though looking for someone. "For God's sake, keep your voice down. All we need is for that old man to hear us and come through the door with gun in hand."

"He's busy on the phone," Julie said when he let her speak again. "Besides, he's old. He doesn't hear very well."

"Why did you hire him, then?"

That was a good question. They'd hired him because he was a retired cop and wanted the job. But Julie didn't answer; was too angry at the moment to bother. How dared he come in here and berate her for trying to help him? She tried to wrench her arm away. "You can let me go now, you know. You don't have to keep holding me."

"No way, lady. I'm not going to let you go. I came all the way over here to find you. The next thing I know you'll be at the police station looking up records."

"Colin, I'm not going to do any such thing. Let me go. All this proves is that you're stronger than me. Is that what you want? Does that make you feel good?"

Colin was so angry with her he was beyond reason. "Believe me, Julie," he answered, "with you, nothing could make me feel good!"

She glared at him. "You seemed to enjoy kissing me the other night. I noticed you had yourself a pretty fun time."

"As I recall you didn't exactly have a terrible time, either," he countered. Then he swore crudely. "Oh, hell." He grabbed her hand and pulled her along. "This is ridiculous. I'm not going to stand here and discuss kissing you, when some old man is sitting up there with a gun. Come on, let's go. Before he figures out we're here."

But their arguments must have been loud enough to have alerted the security guard, for all of a sudden the door to the reception area opened and he peered into the hall.

"Anybody there?"

"It's George," Julie murmured.

Colin pushed her up against a wall. "Quick. Hide."

"Wait. I'll tell him it's me. He won't do anything."

"No." Colin grabbed her. "It's too risky, Julie."

"But he'll let me go. I know he will."

Colin glared. "Julie, the police are looking for you. If he calls them, even for the fun of it, they'll arrest you."

"The police just want to talk to me about my house. Let me tell him it's me."

"No," Colin said firmly. "Julie, your house is not all the police want you for. After I shaved tonight I called Paul." He paused, as if upset. "Along with their knowing it's my cabin, they lifted a set of your fingerprints from the place."

It took a moment for the information to sink in. "Fingerprints? My fingerprints? Are you saying I'm—I'm wanted for murder?"

"I'm afraid so."

Julie didn't have time to think much more about it.

"Hello?" George said again, closer. "Anybody there?"

Thankfully she'd turned out the light. Perhaps with the place dark he'd go away. She could hear his footsteps coming down the hall. Slowly. Pausing. Listening. She huddled against the wall and waited as he went from room to room. *Murder. She was wanted for murder.* She was almost afraid to breathe, afraid he'd hear the frightened rasps from her throat.

All of a sudden she saw a page from the files on the floor. It was white, stark white, in the darkness of the room. The footsteps grew closer. What if he saw it? "Colin?" she whispered, "there's a piece of paper on the floor."

"Shh. There's nothing we can do about it now."

Just then the flashlight beam arced across the room, over the window, the desk. Julie's heart fluttered wildly in her chest and she almost burst with fear. As though realizing she was having problems keeping quiet, Colin placed his hand gently over her mouth. "It's okay," he murmured in her ear. "I'm here, Julie."

She was so scared. She swallowed hard, still holding her breath, waiting for the beam to disappear into the hallway. If George found them it would frighten him. It might even upset him enough that he would accidentally fire his gun. She could hear the clock on her desk, the minutes ticking away slowly, like years. Years she would serve in prison for murder.

Finally the room fell black and the footsteps receded. She nearly collapsed with relief. Her legs trembled and her hands shook, and she sagged against the wall, clutching the files to her chest.

Colin gently grasped her hand. "Come on. Let's go," he murmured. "He's gone back into the other office."

They groped along the hallway into the plant. Their eyes had adjusted to the darkness, so they didn't have much trouble maneuvering. Just as he reached for the door to push it open, she remembered the alarm was flicked on.

"Wait," she warned, but it was too late. Suddenly a siren shrieked a loud warning blast through the plant.

"Damn," he muttered. "Nothing about this place is secure. You can get in the windows, and you've got an alarm that's activated on exit." He pushed her through the door. "Hurry. Run. We've got to reach my car and get out of here."

Julie had found her feet. Fear made them move. And it made her forget any twinge of pain in her ankle. Still clutching the folders, she started across the grass. "Where are you parked?"

"Across the bridge."

The same place he'd parked the other night. Of course. She could still hear the siren shrieking up a storm. Any moment now George would circle from the front and start shooting. From this distance the elderly guard wouldn't be able to identify her.

Colin kept urging her to move faster. It felt strange going down the same hill she'd stumbled on just two nights ago and getting into his car. Because she was holding the folders he opened the door for her and helped her inside, handing her some of the pages she'd dropped. He went around his side and slid in.

They drove away just as George knelt and fired his weapon. The side window shattered and something thudded into the roof. Glass flew all over her lap.

Since they had a head start they were able to avoid the police cars coming to investigate the alarm. Once they got around the corner Colin slowed down and drove at a normal speed.

"Are you all right?" he asked, glancing at her.

She nodded. "Yes, I'm fine. I've just got glass all over me."

"Any cuts?"

"No. Why do you think George fired?"

He arched an eyebrow at the broken window. "Because after the other evening, even if no one else believed you, George was on the alert."

"I knew he could hear a shrieking alarm, but fire a pistol?"

Colin smiled. "You learn something new every day."

"Ain't that the truth."

He turned serious. "Julie, you should know there's an APB out on me. Paul told me the last time I spoke to him. We could be stopped by the police."

"Great. Why are we driving this car?"

"Because I don't have anything else."

She wasn't up to arguing. She leaned forward, trying to straighten the files and brush off the glass from her lap. Papers stuck out at all angles; shards of glass clung to her slacks.

"Just hang on," Colin said. "We'll go to a car wash and vacuum out the glass."

Julie couldn't believe he had the nerve to just pull into a car wash while they were running for their lives, but sure enough, a couple of blocks later, he whipped into a busy station.

The attendant didn't seem to think they were at all strange. Apparently he vacuumed up broken glass all the time. "Did you get hit by a rock?" he asked when Colin opened the door for Julie and she stepped out.

"Yeah," Colin said. "Kids."

"They're always up to something. Did you hear they're dropping bricks off the expressway overpasses these days? We had a guy in here the other day with his windshield broken in."

"Crazy."

When the man was done vacuuming the carpet, Colin took it and ran the hose over Julie's jeans and shirt. "Hold still."

"I'm not a carpet." She felt ridiculous standing in a line of dirty cars on a Sunday night, being vacuumed.

"It's better than being cut."

That was his opinion. She felt even more ridiculous when she realized how he was touching her. Between vacuum strokes he brushed off her breasts, her thighs.

"Turn around." Her backside.

She would have ignored him, except that she felt her nipples peak. Didn't he realize what he was doing? He looked innocent enough, brushing glass from her clothes, but he was a man and she was a woman.

"I'll get it." She pulled away and brushed her sweatshirt and pants off herself. When she looked up she knew he had been aware of every stroke, every touch. She stared at him a long moment. She couldn't help being sarcastic. "What was it you mentioned earlier—that nothing about me could make you feel good?"

"Touché." He glared at her. "Let's go, Julie," he said gruffly.

She smiled as he turned away and handed the attendant a ten-dollar bill. Colin didn't say anything when he slid behind the wheel, and neither did Julie. Although she would have liked to gloat, she figured it was safer not to make him angry. Instead, she studied the scenery as he drove through the city. She'd always thought Chicago was beautiful, impressive night or day. Now the city glittered in the distance like a bright jewel, all lit up and alive. They were almost downtown, when she realized how far they'd gone. "Did you miss the turnoff?" she asked.

"No."

She was confused. "Where are we going?"

"The Bradford."

Julie glanced at him. Because her window was broken, air whipped in, and she thought she hadn't heard him right. "Where?"

"The Bradford Hotel."

That was the most expensive hotel in the city. "For what?"

"To get a room."

"What's the matter with the Uptown Arms?"

"I want a change of scene."

"Just like that you want a change of scene? For the past two days you've stayed in a fleabag hotel, telling me you had to drop out of society, and suddenly you need a change of scene?"

He glanced at her. "You sure can harp. Does that go with your red hair, too?"

"My red hair has nothing to do with it," she said. "You do something totally ridiculous and—"

"Since when is wanting a room in a comfortable hotel ridiculous?" he cut in.

"When you're running for your life. Are you sure this has nothing to do with tonight? I already told you the only reason I left the hotel was that I thought you went to the plant."

"I'm sure."

"You're not making sense, Colin."

"Why?"

"Look at us." She gestured at their clothes, the car. "We can't go to the Bradford Hotel."

"Sure we can."

"Colin, it's not safe. Please don't jeopardize your safety to prove something to me."

"I'm not proving anything to anyone, Julie. I just want a few minutes to go over those files you stole and then I want a good night's sleep on a comfortable bed in a room without bugs or drunks. Tomorrow we make our move."

"Whatever that is," she murmured.

The hotel was just ahead. Julie could see the purple-and-gold uniform of the liveried doorman as he ushered people out of long, sleek limousines into the hotel. She glanced at Colin as he pulled into a parking lot half a block away. He had to be crazy.

But she felt like the crazy one as he escorted her down the street and through the revolving doors so blithely that they might have been a couple of multimillionaires out on the town. A few people in the glass-and-mirror-lined lobby turned and stared, probably at their clothes, but Colin ignored them, going directly to the registration desk and plopping down a major credit card. "A suite, please."

What had gotten into him? Into her? They were running from a murderer. The clerk didn't even question him. Ten minutes later the concierge took them to the elevator and keyed in the penthouse floor. "Have a good night, sir," the man said when the doors slid open silently. "Your suite is to the right and down the hall."

Julie was stunned by the opulent decor as they walked down the thick, carpeted hallway. She'd never been to a concierge level. The glass-and-mirror motif had been carried through up here, too, with skylights and crystal chandeliers gracing the high-lofted ceiling.

"It's beautiful," she murmured when they paused beside their door. They'd been given a corner suite, and it was all the way at the end of the hall. "I can hardly wait to see the room."

Colin glanced back the way they'd come. "Sounds like someone's having a party."

Julie followed his gaze, listening to the loud music. When they passed the room, she noticed the place was smoke filled and crowded. Several people spilled into the hall.

But she was more interested in the suite she was about to share with Colin. Whatever her expectations, it didn't compare with the real thing. When he opened the door and they walked in, she simply stared.

"How much did this cost?" she asked, taking in the fireplace, the plush sofa and chairs. Everything was gold braid and green velvet. Along with a plate of cheese and a bowl of fruit, a box of chocolates and a magnum of champagne sat on a rose-bedecked mahogany desk. More flowers and candy were spread around the room.

"Plenty," Colin answered. He opened the double doors to the bedroom and disappeared inside.

Fascinated, Julie wandered in behind him. The bed was huge, the covers turned down to reveal lacy white pillowcases. More chairs were arranged for intimate conversation. Heavy draperies led to a balcony overlooking the busy street. Because the room was a corner one, it stretched around the side next to a fire escape. She still carried the files and she set them on the bed.

The bathroom was through another set of double doors. It was almost sinfully luxurious, again all glass and mirrors, with a deep green-and-gold-veined marble tub built for two. She could see whirlpool jets set into the shiny surface; bubble bath sat to the side. Huge, fluffy towels in dark green hung on gold racks. Two bathrobes were laid over the steps leading up to the tub and more roses littered the way.

"Everything's so nice you almost hate to disturb it. Are we really going to stay here?"

"Absolutely. We'll check out the whirlpool later. Where are the files?"

Julie turned to the bed. "Over here."

Colin didn't waste much time. As angry as he'd been at her for going to the plant, he seemed awfully glad to get to the information in the files. She started sifting through the personnel files, while he looked through the vouchers she'd taken from Brad's office. At first they didn't say much, just an occasional word or two. Julie had never really scrutinized her employees' histories. She was surprised to discover that one woman had ten grandchildren, and a man in shipping was from Poland.

"Mills & Clark," Colin said. "What kind of company is that?"

Julie frowned. "It's a silver purification company. Why?"

"Norman Osgood owns it."

"What?" She got up and glanced over his shoulder. Sure enough, Norman Osgood's name was at the bottom of several invoices.

"I guess he's not just a pawnbroker, after all. The address listed here is probably his pawnshop's. I'll bet it's closed for business now. You do a lot of business with them?" Colin asked.

She nodded, stunned by the revelation. "They buy some of our silver."

"For what purpose?"

"To purify it."

"Wait a minute." Now Colin frowned. "I thought you reclaimed the silver yourself."

"We do, but it's not pure when we're finished with it. We extract the silver by combining it with another chemical, and it comes out as a compound. Then we sell the compound to another company, where it has to undergo an electrolytic process and then be melted down and poured into bars."

"You don't do that at Lustre?"

"No. The equipment is too expensive. There are only a few companies in the world that can afford the machinery. They get silver from all over. We ship to them daily."

He kept frowning at her. "How? How do you ship the silver?"

"By carrier."

"No, I mean, how—is it in barrels or what? How's the compound packaged when it leaves your plant?"

Julie shrugged. "That depends on what we've extracted the silver from. If it's film, like X-ray film or plain old camera film, the bathwater is treated in a holding tank, and that's what's shipped."

"Do you weigh the tanks? What kind of controls do you use?"

"Actually, we just ship the tanks," she said. "It's an industry norm. They've always been weighed on the other end, at Mills & Clark."

"So you really have no idea how much silver you're extracting."

"Not exactly," Julie admitted. "We have a general idea, though. And we get monthly reports from the company. Usually the tanks are all in the same weight range."

"Which you wouldn't question if a tank was off a gram or two here and there."

"Well, no, we wouldn't question a discrepancy that minor. Not if the report falls within the typical range."

"So in theory, someone could be skimming several grams of silver off each tank. If you ship several tanks a day, that's a lot of silver."

"If that's true, then you're saying Norman Osgood was cheating Lustre, Inc."

"And someone inside may have been helping."

Julie was confused. "But why would he work with someone from Lustre, when he could have the silver all to himself? If he was skimming profits, he wouldn't even have to share."

"Maybe the silver is weighed on your end, after all."

She paused, knowing he had hit on a possibility. "And the person he was working with killed him?"

"Probably."

"Why?"

"Maybe Norm wanted more of a cut. Don't forget what his house looked like. Or maybe the other guy wanted the cut. Usually partnerships like this get ugly, eventually."

Julie paused. "Who do you suppose the other guy or guys are?"

Colin looked at her. "When we find out, we'll find the murderers."

Julie shivered at the thought that someone in her company had committed murder. "But why implicate you? Or me? What does that have to do with it?"

"With me it was a setup. Somebody planned it. I think you came along by accident, a complication the murderer hadn't counted on. You left the building that night at just exactly the right time. The records indicate that two calls went into the dispatcher, yours and another, about five minutes apart."

"You were called there on purpose?"

He nodded. "Someone called me an hour before and told me to meet him at the plant. He hung up before I had a chance to respond. I've got a feeling it was the murderer."

"I'm confused. Was Osgood killed in the parking lot or at some other location?"

Colin's eyes glimmered. Julie was picking up the trade. "Good question. From the body's condition when I got there my best guess is that he was killed about an hour before, or about the time I received the phone call." The body was then deposited in the lot shortly before you and I showed up. I doubt it would be allowed to lie around for an hour before we made our appearances."

"There was a lot of blood, Colin. Are you sure he wasn't killed in the lot?"

Colin shook his head adamantly. "Most of the blood you saw was from Osgood's clothes. The rain made it look fresh, but it wasn't."

"That gets back to the vendetta idea, right? Someone sure carries hard grudges. He wanted to do Osgood in, and he wanted you accused of it." Julie's eyes widened suddenly. "Colin, I just remembered. Brad does all our shipments."

"All of them? You never check on him?"

"Never. That's his job."

Colin thought for a moment. There was only one missing element—his own connection with the murderer. He'd have to think on that. "We might have something, Julie."

"What do we do now, Colin?"

"I don't know. I don't see any other choice but wait until tomorrow. Since everything's pointing to Brad, I think we need to arrange a confrontation."

"Shouldn't we contact the police?"

"Nope. At this point, until we can get the real murderer on more than circumstantial evidence, the case is still an open one."

Julie sighed with a combination of trepidation and eagerness. One more night and it might be all over. Maybe. Brad, of all people. She got up to go into the other room. "I think I'm going to eat some chocolate."

Laughing, Colin placed the files aside and followed her. "That bad, huh? Want to order something from room service?"

"Should we? Won't it be kind of expensive?"

"I intend to pay for it. I've got my credit card."

She smiled and popped a mint into her mouth. "I'll do just fine right here. Want one?"

"No, thanks." He brushed past her to pick up the phone. "You don't want to eat too much of those, you know."

"Why?"

"Too much sugar's no good for you." Pausing a moment, he dabbed a smudge of chocolate from the corner of her mouth. They should both have been prepared for the contact, but they weren't. As he ran his finger across her bottom lip her breath caught in her throat, and she stared up at him. His expression had changed from teasing to intense need.

"Colin? What's wrong?"

He dropped his hand so quickly he might have been burned. He shook his head. "Nothing."

"Something's wrong."

He turned away. Something was wrong, all right, and aside from the fact that they were running from the law like scum, it was that he wanted her. God, he wanted to take her in his arms and carry her to the bed and make mad, passionate love to her. He had never wanted anything so badly in his life. He yearned for her with every fiber of his being.

"Colin, please tell me what's the matter."

"I want you," he said angrily. Perhaps he could shock her, make her angry at him.

But she moved closer. "Oh? Can't that go both ways?"

Colin frowned and shook his head again. "It's wrong, Julie. Go away. Let me alone."

"Why is it wrong?"

All they'd shared was a kiss. One lousy kiss. Yet deep down Colin knew they could so easily have shared more. One touch was all it had taken to ignite the feelings he'd banked since the moment he'd looked at her in his apartment and realized she was the one woman who might steal his heart. They had both been careful not to touch, not to look at each other, to remain neutral. "It's just wrong," he said. "I'm no good for you. Go eat your chocolate."

"I happen to like sugar, Colin. It hasn't hurt me yet."

He spun around to face her. "But I could. Dammit, Julie, you're not ready for what I'm feeling."

She faced him squarely. "Yes, I am. In fact, I've been ready for what you're feeling for a long time."

"It's been only two days."

She shrugged. "What does it matter how long we've known each other? We both want the same thing. We both feel the same thing."

"I don't want to hurt you, Julie."

"How can you hurt me by kissing me?"

"Julie, please don't do this." He couldn't resist much longer.

"I'm not going to move, Colin. Kiss me," she said huskily. "Kiss me the way you did before."

"I'm having a heck of a time keeping my hands off of you."

She licked her lips once. Nervously? Sensuously. Then she shrugged again. "So don't."

"If I touch you I won't stop." Her lips were mere inches from his. He caressed her cheek gently, running his thumb along her jaw.

"Good."

By now they were both breathing hard. Colin let his thumb trail across her mouth, outlining her lips. All he'd wanted when he'd come here was a moment to read the files and a good night's sleep. He shouldn't have let things escalate, but they had, and he couldn't hold back anymore.

Nearly choking with need, he pulled her to his body and kissed her with all his pent-up passion. Julie gasped and swayed her hips into his, circling her arms around his neck. When he twisted his fingers in her hair the heavy mass tumbled down around her shoulders. Somehow they reached the bed, peeling off their own clothes as they sank onto it. Julie knew he was going to make love to her, now, right this moment, and she was glad. It was inevitable, as day followed night, summer came after spring. She'd known it all along. That tension that tore at her belly and raged in her blood had always been there. It was time to appease the beast.

"You're sure?" was the only thing he said to her as he caressed her heated skin. His hands were everywhere at once, on her breasts, teasing their swollen peaks, trailing down her stomach, drawing circles on the insides of her thighs, finally coming to rest in her moist warmth. He kissed her all over, too, his mouth and tongue working magic.

"Yes, I'm sure," she murmured, meeting him touch for touch, stroke for stroke. "You know I'm not your type."

"I know."

"Love me, Colin."

And then she was lost as he pulled her to him and began a slow, tortuous rhythm that matched her own. With each movement the storm within her gathered strength, raging into an uncontrolled whirlwind of need. She felt battered by its intensity. At the height of desire, she clutched his arms as he held her, wanting more, yet needing to pull away because the pleasure was so intense. She cried out as the storm broke. Waves of contentment rolled over her.

Spasms of intense pleasure gripped him at the same moment, and he collapsed. "Oh, God, Julie."

It took Colin a few minutes to move. When he mustered strength, he rolled over, pulling her with him and resting her head on his shoulder. With a sigh he brushed back her sweat-dampened hair and kissed her forehead gently. "Kind of wild, huh?"

"Very."

"Are you all right?"

An odd question. She was so weak she didn't know if she could move. She felt as if she'd just died and come back to life, an odd yet pleasurable experience. She'd never felt anything like it. "Yes, I'm fine," she answered him simply.

"Was it good for you?"

She flushed. She'd always had trouble talking about intimate details, admitting her innermost thoughts. And this was the most intimate time between a man and woman. Yet she felt easy with him, comfortable. "It was very good."

"It was good for me, too."

She was glad. She glanced up at him and traced her finger over his lips. They were soft and full, such a contrast to his hard body. "I pleased you?" she asked softly. "I'm not very experienced."

"Believe me, Julie, you did fine." They were lying side by side on the bed. She shifted, and he picked up several strands of her hair and sifted them through his fingers, letting them fall in layers. "Your hair is beautiful. It looks like fire."

"I wish I'd known you when I was a teenager," she said, smiling at him.

"Rough?"

"I was always getting teased. I still get teased a lot." Not knowing what to do with her knee, she placed it on his leg. His rough hairs prickled her sensuously.

"Well, I think you're gorgeous, red hair and all."

She glanced at him with a frown. "Really?"

"Absolutely."

She placed her hand on his forehead as if testing for a fever. "I have frizzy red hair, a complexion that sunburns, lips that are too wide, and my teeth never quite straightened right. And my sister says my breasts are too big."

"She's jealous. Sounds perfect to me."

She laughed. "Maybe. But I am afraid of bugs."

He paused for a moment. "Now that's a problem."

"Not anymore," she countered. "If you look in the closet at the Uptown Arms you'll see that the little suckers are all dead, lying on their backs with their legs sticking up in the air."

"I never realized you were so brutal, Julie."

"I'm one tough momma."

He laughed, amused. "You're tough, but I'm not sure about momma."

"Little do you know. A kid on the street called me that tonight."

He pulled back and glared at her in mock anger. "I'm still angry at you for that little stunt, you know. You could have gotten hurt. The streets down there are rough."

"I wish you'd be consistent. Are those people humanity or the dregs of humanity?"

"Don't be smart, Julie."

"I'm sorry, Colin. I really did think you'd left."

"You know I wouldn't leave you."

She was amazed at how different he was now. Perhaps he wasn't, though. Perhaps she was the different one, now that she wasn't fighting him. She traced her finger from his lips to his nose. "How did you get this?"

"Football. I broke it. A linebacker fell on me."

"And this?" She moved down to trace the scar under his jaw.

"I fell off a tractor at the old onion farm."

She wondered what story lay behind that remark. One day she'd ask. One day soon. "I thought you might have been shot when you were a cop."

"I was," he said.

She touched the scar on his flank. "Here?"

"Yes."

"Were you very sick?"

"I was in the hospital a few days."

"What happened?" For some reason it was important for her to know. She needed to know things about him. He knew so much about her, her innermost thoughts, her habits, her quirks.

"I was involved in a shoot-out," he said. "A street gang barricaded themselves in an old building and were threatening to kill people one by one. I was wearing a vest, but the bullet hit me just below it."

"Is that why you quit the police force?"

"No. I quit the force because I kept seeing injustice, and it ate at me."

"So you solve cases yourself now."

He nodded. "Whatever ones I get. That's enough talk about me. Tell me about Julie Hunter."

He had been running his fingers along her side absently as he spoke. The simple gesture had aroused her. Every nerve ending in her body felt on fire. "Why talk at all?" she murmured as his hand slid up to her breast. "It's late. We should get some sleep."

He laughed, pulling the covers over both of them. "Excellent idea."

THE POUNDING AT THE DOOR startled Julie. She sat up and brushed her hair out of her eyes, trying to get her bearings. They had fallen asleep late. The gray light filtering into the room told her it was almost dawn.

Colin had already sprung from the bed. "Who is that?" she whispered. "What's going on?"

Colin scowled. "I don't know. But I'd be willing to bet it's not a social call. You'd better get dressed."

The urgency in his tone frightened her more than the pounding. She grabbed her clothes and started pulling them on as the pounding continued. Then a loud, ugly voice boomed out, "Open up. Police."

Chapter Eleven

"Damn!" Colin muttered. "Of all things, the police."

Julie stared at the bedroom door, paralyzed by fear. "What do they want?"

"I don't know. Someone must have reported us."

"Did you use your real name with the hotel clerk?"

"Unfortunately," he answered, starting to throw on his clothes, too. "But I didn't have a choice. I used a credit card to get the room, and certainly didn't think the police had enough time to contact hotels about us. Maybe the airports, but not hotels. Damn," he muttered again. "I sure don't need to get arrested now. Not when we're so close to solving the murder. Quick. We've got to get the files and get out of here before they break down the door."

The police were still pounding and shouting, wanting in. Julie didn't argue. If the authorities got in they could confiscate the files—their only evidence—and arrest them. Once they were identified, it would be all over.

Hurriedly she pulled on her things, snapping her bra and struggling with her socks. She was breathless with the fear of getting caught. "How are we going to get out of here?"

"The fire escape."

"The..." Even the thought was horrifying. "Colin, that's at the side of the building. On the outside. I can't go down that. We're fifteen stories up."

"Would you rather stay and get arrested?" Now that he had dressed, he grabbed the files from where they'd left them on the floor and stuffed them in the plastic garbage bag lining the wastebasket. She slipped on her clothes in the meantime. Not even looking to see if she was ready, he tucked them under his arm and pulled at her hand. "Let's go." Just as he spoke the door to the sitting room crashed open. "Hurry."

They slipped out onto the balcony. The early-morning air felt cold on her heated skin and she shivered. Colin wedged a chair leg against the sliding door, hoping to deter the police. Juggling the bag of files, he grabbed her hand again and pulled her toward the side balcony. The fire escape was a full ten feet away across a gap.

"Are we going to jump?" Julie asked, already knowing the answer to her question. It was the only choice.

"Yes. I'll go first. When I get over I'll catch you."

Her mistake was in glancing down. She looked at the ground and the fire escape, then back at the ground, and her stomach sank. Since the balcony didn't overlook Michigan Avenue, there wasn't any traffic below, but she could see an alley. The cement there was just as hard as on the street. "Colin, I can't do this."

"Sure, you can. You're tough, Julie."

"I might be tough, but I wasn't meant for this kind of life. I don't like turmoil."

He laughed. *Laughed*, in the middle of such strife. "Want some more chocolate? I'll buy you a candy bar later."

"How did you know that?"

"I know a lot about you. Why do you think you like sugar? It's just like danger. Gives you a high." When the bedroom door crashed open, he glanced over his shoulder. His expression sobered. "Hurry, Julie, they're coming." Suddenly he shoved her in front of him toward the railing. "You're going to have to go first." When she continued to hesitate, he said, "It's going to be all right. Trust me."

But it wasn't all right. Just as she climbed up onto the railing, she heard the crash of glass—the balcony door being broken open. "Oh, God, I don't want to climb the Himalayas anymore."

"Is that something you wanted to do?"

"Yes," she murmured. "I also wanted to float in the Dead Sea. Now I just want to stay alive."

"Then go," Colin urged. "Jump!"

Fear was the only thing that could have propelled her across the space. In one quick movement, she hurled herself through the air and fell on the other side, landing sideways on her foot. She groaned inwardly, wincing from the pain.

As if realizing it was too late for him to make it, Colin tossed her the bag of files. "Look, Julie, one of us has got to stay free. If you hurry you can get away, and they won't know we were together. I'm going around to the other side of the balcony to stall them."

"Colin—"

"Listen to me," he said. "This is important. You've got to get out of here. Get down the fire escape and get the car." He tossed her his wallet. "Here's some money. Go to my sister's. I'll meet you there. Wait for me. And for God's sake, stay away from the plant," he added ominously.

Before she could utter a word, he slipped around the corner of the balcony out of view. "Please be careful," she mouthed toward his disappearing figure, and with one final glance, she started down the fire escape. The sound of more glass crashing, the police coming out on the balcony, Colin being found, loud voices, his being arrested, reached her ears. She glanced back once, thinking that surely the police would see her. He must have managed to keep them on that side of the balcony, because no one spotted her. She kept going down. At the bottom the steps ran out. What good was a fire escape that didn't go all the way to the ground? She would have to leap down. It was jump or be arrested—perhaps shot, if someone noticed her. There had to be police cars all over in front of the building.

Knowing her ankle was reinjured, she dropped the files to the ground. Then, hanging on to the metal rung, she closed her eyes and fell, landing most of her weight on her good foot. She was surprised she didn't have any broken bones when she stood up and dusted herself off. She felt proud. She could do this. In a way she wanted to call out to Colin and let him know she'd made it, but she couldn't. That would tip everyone off. Clutching the files in her arms, she hurried down the alley. There had been a twinge of pain when she landed and her ankle was sore, but she could still use her foot. She had to. She had to get to his sister's. A squad car came up the alley the other way just as she rounded the corner and headed for the parking garage. She could hear sirens in the distance, and a paddy wagon passed by.

What if he didn't get out of jail?

But she knew he would. She had to believe he would. She'd gotten away, hadn't she? Funny, her success felt kind of anticlimactic. So what if she'd made it? He was in danger.

THE POLICE WASTED NO TIME in arresting Colin for the murder of Norman Osgood. Not wanting Julie to get caught, he'd struggled briefly, trying to take their minds off her—if, in fact, they'd even known she was with him. Once they had him in handcuffs, they led him back through the broken doors into the hotel bedroom.

"How'd you know I was here?" he asked when a big, burly detective shoved him down on the bed. The man was dressed in plainclothes—a suit and a tie—and he was full of swagger and outrage.

"We got an anonymous tip from a concerned citizen."

So that was how. Perhaps they had been tailed all this time, despite his precautions. At least the tipster hadn't mentioned Julie. Which confirmed his suspicions that he was the target all along. He hoped she got to his sister's all right. "Where are you taking me?"

"Where else? The station house. You should know the procedure, Marshall." He jerked Colin up and pushed him forward. Several other policemen fell in formation both in front and behind him. "Don't worry, you're not going to get away."

"I hadn't intended to."

"Too bad."

Obviously the detective had a Dirty Harry complex. But Colin didn't say anything as they rode down the elevator and went out the door. He was stuffed inside a paddy wagon. The vehicle smelled of vomit and urine and dirty bodies, but he ignored that, too. He had to concentrate on how he was going to get out of jail so he could confront Brad Davies and clear himself of murder. Unfortunately murderers didn't get to post bail, at least not for a good long time, even with top-notch legal counsel, and particularly not with an ironclad case against them. The police not only had fingerprints, they had a corpse, and now they had the murder weapon.

Just as Colin was led into the interrogation room at the station, the detective who had arrested him slapped the Grizzly on the table and looked at him. "You carry a big gun, man."

Colin smiled. "The better to shoot you with."

"I hate smart asses."

"I bet you'd love a confession."

"It'd make my day easier."

"I'll bet."

"Not going to talk?"

Colin shook his head. "Not on your life, buddy. Not until I see my lawyer."

The detective scowled, and his mouth twisted into a sneer. "You former cops are all alike, aren't you? You think you can commit any damned crime you want and get away with it just because you used to be in the department. I don't like cops gone bad, and I particularly don't like you. You give the whole lot of us a rotten rap." He wrinkled his nose. "You stink, Colin Marshall."

Colin just shrugged. It would be foolish to fight. That's what the detective wanted; the turkey was itching to slug someone. Apparently things hadn't changed much. The job was still frustrating. "Whether you like me or not, I have rights, buddy, even if I am a cop gone bad. After you get my lawyer, we'll see who stinks."

"You know damned well your lawyer won't get here for four more hours."

Colin slid down in his chair and crossed his arms over his chest as though relaxing. He smiled again. "I'm not going anywhere."

Although the detective looked murderous, he slammed out of the room. Since they couldn't interrogate him, the police spent the time fingerprinting him and booking him for murder. Ironically he was at the station house he used to work out of. His desk sat across the room. Paul came in about eight.

"What the hell?" His ex-partner stood staring at Colin. Then he frowned as he walked over to his side. "How'd you get caught?"

"Hotel."

Paul shook his head. "Broads'll get you every time."

The remark irritated Colin. "It was Julie. And we were at the hotel to look at files."

"Oh, I see." Paul grinned. But Colin didn't. He glared at the man standing across from him. Uncomfortable, Paul shifted. "She must be one awfully special lady."

"She is."

"Okay, guy, how are you going to get out of this one?"

Colin shrugged. "I don't know. Right now I'm waiting for my lawyer. Got any ideas?"

"No ideas, but I've got a puzzle. You know those old cars you wanted me to look up? I was going down the list of owners and there's one listed for an Amy Walker."

"Who the devil is Amy Walker? Is she employed at Lustre?"

"Nope. But of all the owners of antique Cadillac cars listed with the local clubs, she's the only one without an address listing in any of our computer files or the phone book. We tried to tie in the others with Lustre, but as far as we can tell, none of them lives or works near the place. They're dealers, a few executives, and at least one university professor."

"So can you run up something on her, this Amy Walker?"

"Sure, we're working on it now."

"Good." Colin shook his head. "Look, Paul, I'm really in a bind here. Julie's supposed to go to my sister's. Can you give Gayle a call to make sure she made it?"

"Sure." Paul went toward a phone. "Hang in there. I'll be right back. Oh, by the way," he went on, pausing, "we have some leads on where Roger was that Friday. But the rundown won't be in till late this afternoon, if then."

Colin nodded. As far as he was concerned Roger was clean. At the moment Brad was his prime suspect. "Great. Just get ahold of Julie."

BY THE TIME JULIE ARRIVED in the northwest suburbs, she was certain Colin could never get away from the police and meet her at his sister's. Why had she left him? They would put him in jail and throw away the key. She knew they had arrested him for murder. *Murder.* If only she could do something to help him. But what? She needed time to think, to plan.

The sun had come up, and the day promised to be hot and humid, typical summer weather for Chicago. Even though it was Monday morning, traffic was light, since she was going against it, and she made good time. It was a good thing, because she was low on gas. She pulled into his sister's driveway just as a man, Gayle's husband, presumably, pulled out. Wind had rushed in through the broken window as she'd driven, wreaking havoc with her hair, and considering how quickly she'd dressed, she'd probably scared every person she passed along the way, but she got out of the car and ran to the door.

Colin's sister answered the doorbell dressed in a robe and slippers. Brutus pranced beside her, barking and running around, excited. He had certainly gotten over his drugging. The kids were screaming. Julie didn't know quite what to say. She stood in the doorway clutching the files, hoping she didn't seem like some kind of madwoman, but certain that if she did, she was in the right place. Everything was in turmoil. In addition to the dog, three little kids ran around screaming and yelling and playing.

"Good morning." She tried to talk over the noise. "I don't know if you remember me, but I'm Julie Hunter. I was with Colin the other night."

Gayle shook her head. "Oh, no, he can't do this—he can't do this to me. I can't get involved again. I *won't* get involved."

"Look," Julie said, "he's in trouble. I'm in trouble, too. You've got to help us."

"No. I can't." The woman was practically in tears. "Oh, God, why me? Always. Always he puts me through these messes. Now he's brought the dog."

"Look, I'll take the dog," Julie said. "If you'll just help me. We need your help."

"Is it his cloak-and-dagger stuff?"

"Yes."

"I wish he'd stop it."

"He's not going to. It's his life-style."

Gayle looked at her more sympathetically, yet still cautious. "What kind of trouble is he in?"

"He's in jail."

"God." The woman sighed, obviously frustrated. "What do I have to do?"

Julie gestured at the files. "Just let me stay here and wait for him. I need to make a couple of phone calls." She would call his ex-partner, Paul. That is, if she could find his name in the phone book.

Gayle continued to hesitate. One of the kids, a little towheaded toddler, came to the door and clung to her leg, just staring at Julie with his thumb planted in his mouth. Brutus stood there and whined, wagging his stubby tail. Then all of a sudden the cat appeared, and the dog started growling and barking, obviously torn between wanting to chase the cat and needing to keep everyone inside the house. The little boy gave a whoop and ran through the room after the kitten. The effect was worse than total bedlam.

"Lord, I can't stand this." Gayle was obviously at her wit's end. "Okay," she said, pushing her hair back off her face, "I'll help you, but you have to take the dog. You can't back out of that."

Julie nodded. "Deal."

Brutus calmed down some when Julie got inside the house. After giving up on the cat, he flopped down on the floor and whined at her. But she wasn't concerned about the dog. She had to figure out a way to help Colin. By now she was convinced that the police would have him in the electric chair unless she did something. That something was to confront Brad herself.

Gayle didn't think she should do it. Once things had calmed down, the woman was actually kind of nice, and she'd listened to the entire story with a kind of morbid fascination. "I don't think going to the plant is going to help Colin at all," his sister said. "In fact, all it will do is put you in danger. If this man Brad is guilty, won't he try to kill you?"

Julie paced back and forth across the living room floor. Somewhere along the way she'd lost her barrette and she was back to shoving her hair out of her eyes.

"I'm not sure, but I don't think Brad will hurt me. And even if he does, I have to do something. Colin is sitting there in jail." The more she thought about it, the more she realized she couldn't just stand there and talk. "I'm going. What have I got to lose?"

"Your life."

Julie shrugged. For the past two days she'd risked her life over and over. Decision made, she grabbed the files and started for the door. Brutus beat her there, but she paused. "Can I borrow your car? Colin's is almost out of gas."

"I really don't think this is a smart idea."

"Please?"

Gayle was easily convinced. Julie was certain that was why Colin took such advantage of her. His sister sighed. "I hate making snap decisions. If Colin comes here he's going to be angry at me for letting you go."

"So?"

"He's my brother."

"He brought you the cat and the dog."

Gayle thought about that for a moment. "You're right." She got up from the sofa. "I'll get the keys." She rushed into the kitchen as though hurrying before she could change her mind. She came back with her purse, grabbed a set of keys from it and tossed them to Julie. "The car's in the garage. I'll open it while you get the dog. You will take the dog, won't you? You promised."

Julie smiled. "How do I get him?"

"Now that's a problem," his sister said. "Wait here. I'll find the leash, then you lead him out."

Gayle appeared a moment later, Brutus's familiar leash in her hand. The rottweiler pranced around, knowing he was about to be let out. At the front door, a relieved Gayle turned to Julie and smiled. "You know, I think I'm going to like you."

"Me, too," Julie said. On sudden impulse, she hugged Gayle. Then she ran quickly down the steps, Brutus just behind her. She had to hurry. She had to do something to get Colin out of jail.

PAUL MISSED JULIE by seconds. He hung up the phone and headed back to the interrogation room. Once inside, he dismissed the policeman who was guarding Colin.

"What's the matter?" Colin asked when the blue-uniformed cop closed the door and left.

"She's gone."

Colin frowned. "What?"

"Julie was there," Paul explained, "but Gayle said she left a few minutes ago."

"Damn! Where the dickens did she go? Did Gayle say?"

Paul nodded. "She was going to the plant. She wants to get you out of jail, so she's decided to talk to Brad herself."

"Damn!" Colin swore again. If he got his hands on her he'd strangle her. "Look, Paul—" He glanced around. No one was guarding him, but there was a two-way mirror and a microphone. If someone was looking or listening they were both dead. "I need your help. I've got to get to her. She's in danger. Give me your gun."

"What?" The man was incredulous. "Come on, Colin. Think. If I give you my gun, I'll get fired. I don't mind helping you, man, but this is too much."

"You won't get fired," Colin assured him. "I'm going to hit you. I'll try not to make it hard."

His ex-partner frowned. "Gee, thanks."

"Look, I've got to get out of here, and the only way I can do it is to overpower you. When you go down, stay down. As far as they'll know I tried to escape. You tried to stop me, I took your gun and knocked you out."

"Colin—" he started to protest.

"Paul, how long have you known me? She's going to get herself killed."

"I'll send a squad. We'll get somebody out to the plant."

"To do what? The cops won't arrest Brad. They don't have anything to arrest him on, and she's going to get hurt. Dammit, I have to go."

"You get yourself in such jams. Colin, I can't—"

Though he hated to do it, Colin swung midsentence. Since Paul wasn't expecting it, his head snapped back and he fell to the floor. Maybe it was a good thing he was knocked out. Colin knelt beside the man and felt for a pulse. Assured Paul was all right, he grabbed the gun. Knowing he had only a few seconds, he threw a chair at the window. There were bars on the outside, so he couldn't get out that way, but the broken glass would indicate a scuffle. On his way out of the room, he tipped over a table.

When he opened the door all hell broke loose. People came running from all over the station house. But Colin wielded the .45 automatic expertly. And why not? He'd carried one for years. "Anybody moves and he's dead," he said, emphasizing his statement by waving everyone to the side with the gun. "I've got eight rounds and I won't miss."

"You're crazy," the detective who arrested him said.

"Maybe." Colin crept along with his back to the wall. "I'm leaving and I don't expect any trouble. Is there a squad out front? Well?" Colin demanded when no one answered. He aimed the weapon and cocked it.

"Yes," the detective answered grudgingly. "There's a squad out front."

Colin nodded. "As I remember, this is a busy precinct. I wouldn't shoot if I were you. An innocent bystander could get hurt."

The detective nearly spit on the floor. "You slime. You're a pox on the entire force."

"Sorry you feel that way, buddy." Whether the man liked it or not, Colin had to help Julie. Brad was a killer. Why he wanted to hurt Colin wasn't clear, but at this point that didn't matter. "Maybe one day you'll understand."

"Don't count on it. If I catch you, you're a dead man."

And if he didn't leave, Julie was a dead woman. Colin smiled. "*If* you catch me."

Then he spun around and ran out the door.

Chapter Twelve

Brutus sat in the front seat of the car and nearly grinned as they pulled into morning traffic. Julie tried not to speed. All she needed was to be stopped by the police. But she was so anxious to find Brad and make him confess she accelerated nevertheless. She had already decided to use the small hand-held tape recorder she used to dictate letters into so she could record Brad's confession. Brutus would be her muscle, if things turned nasty, and George would be there, as well as the other employees who would be trickling in throughout early morning hours.

When she took a corner nearly on two wheels she realized she had to slow down. She was beginning to drive like Colin.

"Almost," she murmured to the dog, and pumped the brakes. "Almost blew it."

Brutus whined in answer.

She turned down a couple of more streets. The industrial park was already busy with Monday-morning truck traffic and cars of employees headed for various businesses. At last she whipped into the parking lot of Lustre, Inc. Odd, how things looked so peaceful. Yet the past two days she'd learned how deceptive appearances could be. Virgil's truck was there. So was George's old car. Except for a few other automobiles, the rest of the lot was empty. There'd be a lot of activity that afternoon, though, when trucks pulled in to pick up the silver that had been processed that day. In the light of day the trees didn't look at all eerie. A soft breeze rustled the leaves. She glanced at her watch. She'd forgotten how early it was. Brad wouldn't be in before ten. And she'd been in a hurry.

She parked the car anyhow and headed for the building. Not knowing what to do with the dog, she grabbed his leash and took him along. George was ready to leave. He stood talking to Virgil, probably relating the excitement of last night. When she walked inside the front door he glanced at her in surprise.

"Miss Hunter. You're here. You're all right. Brad said you lost your house to a fi—" Just then the security guard noticed the dog. His eyes grew wide with fear. "Oh, dear."

"Don't worry, he won't hurt you." She couldn't help smiling. Not only had she had a fire, she'd been shot at—by him! She placed the bag of files on the desk. "I'm fine, George. How are you?"

"I'm just great. I don't know if the old ticker's gonna survive all the excitement, though. I was just telling Virgil about the attempted robbery last night. They didn't get any silver. I made sure of that. Then I called the cops. Since there was nothing missing they took a report. Damnedest things going on, though, that's for sure, what with you seeing that body and having the fire and all."

"Yes, things are kind of odd."

"You gonna work today?"

It kept coming home to her that she was dressed oddly. "No, I was just passing by. I'm still trying to get things sorted out with the fire and all."

Virgil frowned at Brutus, who sat obediently beside her. "Where'd you get the dog?"

"He belongs to a friend. I know Brad's car isn't out front," Julie went on, "but he wouldn't be in by any remote chance, would he?"

Virgil was the one who answered. He laughed. "You expect Brad before ten?"

"I hoped there might be an offside chance."

"What do you need to see him about?"

"A few things." All of a sudden Julie wondered if Virgil would know about the shipping policy. She glanced at him. "Could I talk to you for a minute before everyone comes in?"

He shrugged. "Sure. I want to get the vats going, though, before everyone gets here. Is the back okay?"

"Fine."

George waved to them. "Well, I'll be going then, since you're both here and you won't be needing me."

"Fine," Julie answered.

"Take care. Watch out for those burglars now. Won't anybody be in for a while."

Virgil led the way toward the factory area. Julie scooped up the files and followed, leading the dog along beside her. She would return them and extract the tape recorder from a side drawer later. "You'd better tie him up," Virgil said, meaning the dog. "He might knock something over."

"Good idea." She hooked the end of the leash over the doorknob as Virgil started hosing cyanide into a vat.

"What's in the bag? Looks like an awfully big lunch."

She took a deep breath, hoping she was right. Should she tell him? She needed all the help she could get, and she knew Virgil was in on many of the company's systems; in fact, he'd played a hand in developing some of them. "Files," she answered at last. "Virgil, you wouldn't happen to know if Brad knew a Norman Osgood, would you?"

He screwed up his forehead, considering. He started rounding the vat, checking the valves, and Julie couldn't see his face. "The name's not familiar. Why?"

"I think Brad killed him." she said softly.

"What?" Virgil asked from behind a vat, his voice echoing through the plant. He stepped into view, wiping his hands methodically as if they were dirty, a strange look on his face. Julie interpreted it as shock and puzzlement.

"Look, I know it sounds crazy, Virgil, but I think Brad is skimming off profits. The robbery last night wasn't a robbery—it was me." She spoke softly and patted the files. "It's all in here. Brad's the one who makes out the invoices. We've been losing money steadily for years with the silver that's shipped to Osgood's company."

"Why would Brad do that?" Virgil asked, his eyes glowing unbelievingly.

"I don't know."

"Sure is hard to believe. What are you going to do about it?"

"Wait for him. I'm going to confront him with the evidence, record his reaction."

Virgil moved around behind her, going for a gas mask fixed to some of the vat piping that jutted out at all angles from the metal containers lining the room. "I don't know, Miss Hunter. You ought to call the police. If what you say is true, you're in a dangerous position." His voice was low, slow.

"It's true," Julie answered. "It's just so hard to believe. If it wasn't for the files, I wouldn't have known. And the fact that he was at my house just before the explosion." She sat there talking, not paying attention to what Virgil was doing, when all of a sudden he appeared behind her and clamped his hand over her mouth.

"Okay," he said in a menacingly low voice, "game's up, Miss Hunter. Place the files on the floor and come with me."

Confused, Julie started to struggle. "What are you doing?"

"Where's Marshall?"

"Colin's in jail," she answered, suddenly realizing the answer to her own question.

"How much does he know?"

"Everything. Virgil, you're the last person I would have doubted. What are you doing?"

He shoved her toward the cyanide hose. The dog had started barking, but since the leash was hooked on the doorknob, he couldn't get away. "I'm taking care of you once and for all," Virgil said, ripping the bag from her hands. "And then I'm going after Marshall."

"You're going to kill me? That's stupid. Why would you risk your freedom—your life—for Brad?"

Virgil just gave her an evil smile and shook his head in disappointment. "It's not Brad who's shipping that silver, Miss Hunter." He spit as he dragged her across the room. "It's me. Brad just makes out the invoices. I send them out. He never played any part in the scheme."

"You?" She was stunned. She stumbled along behind him. "You've been shipping the silver? It was you alone?"

"Of course it was me. I'm the only one around here who has the brains. Besides, why do you think Brad would have to steal? He doesn't even get his hands dirty."

The dog kept barking up a storm, but Julie was more concerned with Virgil. "You've been stealing all along?"

He took the cyanide hose in one hand and placed the gas mask over his mouth with the other. "Yes, with a greedy pawnbroker who got greedier. And I'm not going to get caught now. Nobody's here but you and me. And nobody's going to be here for several hours. We're the early birds," he said with a laugh. "Getting rid of you will be easy. After you're dead, I'm going to come in and find you. The dog knocked over the cyanide hose. He'll be dead, as well," Virgil said, his voice sounding hollow as it came through the mask. "Too bad you couldn't leave things alone, Miss Hunter. Too bad you had to keep poking your nose around. Bastard sent me to jail."

Everything was coming into focus. "Colin? Colin sent you to jail?"

"I spent five lousy years in Menard State Prison," he answered, "all because of Colin Marshall."

"What did you do?"

"It doesn't matter. I shouldn't have been caught. But your cop friend was Johnny-on-the-spot. Actually, maybe it does matter," Virgil went on derisively, the gas mask distorting his words eerily. "I got sent up for manslaughter. Do you know what manslaughter is, Miss Hunter?"

It was murder. As he held the cyanide hose toward her, Julie panicked. He was stronger than she was, and since he had on the mask, the gas wouldn't affect him.

She started struggling harder. "No, don't do this, Virgil."

He laughed again. "You're not getting away, not now."

But she grabbed the mask from his face and tossed it into a corner. She twisted from him, pushing him backward, and ran to the door. The dog was making a terrible racket. Not wanting to leave the animal, she grabbed the leash and pulled him along. Thinking it all a fun game, he scampered along beside her. Virgil reached for her just as Colin came in the door.

The plant manager stopped dead in his tracks. So did Julie. "Colin! How did you get out of jail?"

"I broke out." He had spent the past half hour trying to get there as fast as he could, first hot-wiring a car, then outracing squad-cars with lights and sirens on. Everybody and his brother had been chasing him. But he'd managed to lose them. Now he paused and glanced at Virgil, and suddenly he knew the connection. "Well, I'll be damned."

"Yes, you will," the plant manager answered. "Finally figured it out, huh? Well, goody for you. What are you doing here, Marshall?"

"I came to get Julie. It looks like I've found a murderer, though."

"Think so?"

"Colin—"

He pushed her behind him. "I haven't got time to talk right now, Julie. Just stay back."

The two men faced off, circling each other warily.

"Let him go, Colin," she said, knowing they were going to fight. "It's not worth getting killed."

"Get back, Julie, there's nothing you can do."

As she looked at the two men she realized the truth of that statement. If there was a fight the plant manager would have the advantage of weight. He was much stockier than Colin, built like a prizefighter.

"Coming here won't do you any good," the plant manager said. "You'll never pin this on me. It'll never stick. The body was found in your cabin, and Osgood was shot with your gun."

"As soon as I take the records we found to the police that story will change. Give it up, Thompson."

Virgil flashed that menacing smile again. "I'm not going to give anything up. Not on your life. You want me, you're going to have to kill me." With that he slipped a knife from his boot and flipped it open in one quick motion. The blade glinted ominously in the fluorescent light. "That is, if I don't kill you first."

"No!" Julie shouted, starting forward. "Colin, don't—"

This time Colin didn't glance her way. Knowing he had to watch Virgil's every move, he never flicked his eyes from the man.

"Get out of here," he said to her in a low, tight tone. "Take the dog with you."

Brutus hadn't stopped barking. Julie held him. "No, I won't leave. Colin, please, don't fight him. Let the police handle it. You said they were following you."

"The cops won't take me, either," Virgil declared. "I'm not going back to prison."

"Then give up," Colin said.

Virgil laughed. The sound was diabolical as it echoed in the large room. "You know me better than that, Marshall. Come on," he taunted, waving his hand, "come and fight me. We'll make a deal. The winner walks away."

"What kind of deal did you make with Norman Osgood?" Colin asked, trying to buy time, wait for an opportunity. "Did you blackmail him or did he blackmail you?"

Virgil laughed again. "That two-bit pawnbroker? What do you think? I made him wealthy. Five years ago he was nothing. I needed a conduit for silver. He needed goods for his store. He practically begged me to finance his new purification plant. The pawnshop was the perfect front for selling silver bars to anyone who'd pay the right price. And believe me there are plenty."

"But Osgood got greedy?" Colin asked, glancing around him for a weapon.

"Always smart Marshall, weren't you?"

"What about your wife, Virgil? Why'd you involve her? You did involve her, didn't you? How else could you be at Julie's and my place almost at the same time?"

The plant manager didn't seem to mind the harassment. He smiled. "It's amazing how a little money spoils a woman. She got used to it. That's how she got involved. What's it to you, anyway?"

"It's nothing to me. I just wondered what kind of sicko could mix his wife up in murder. A friend discovered an antique Cadillac registered in the name of Amy Walker. He thought it was strange, because she was the only owner who wasn't listed in the phone book. It occurred to me on the way over here that perhaps she had registered the car in her maiden name. Her married name might be something like Thompson."

Virgil flashed his grin. "You're too good Colin, you know that? You ought to be a private eye."

As she listened, Julie's heart hammered in fear. Virgil was dangerous. Sick and dangerous. She could tell he would do anything to get out of the mess he was in, including killing the man she loved. She had to do something. Somehow she had to get the police. If she could alert someone, if she could get to the button on the wall, it would automatically sound an alarm. It was usually used to summon the fire department for a chemical leak, but the police always came with the fire department. And it was all she could think of.

She knew Colin had a gun; she saw it when he walked in. But she also knew he wouldn't pull it in a room filled with cyanide vats. Besides, the way Virgil held the knife, one move on Colin's part and the plant manager would throw it. She had no doubt he would come up on the mark; they stood only a few feet apart.

The two of them still circled each other. Julie started to shuffle her way along the wall, trying not to disturb their concentration. It was so quiet she could hear herself breathing. Whining occasionally, still wondering what was going on, Brutus followed her, his nails tip-tapping softly on the floor.

She was almost at the button, when Virgil noticed her. His glance at her was brief, angry. "You touch it and I throw this thing," he threatened. "Your new acquaintance will be history."

"Don't do anything to jeopardize yourself, Julie," Colin told her. "Just stay back."

Virgil must have been growing impatient. "Come on, Marshall," he said, "let's get this over with. Go ahead and make the first move."

Julie knew Colin wouldn't be so foolish as to be sucked into that kind of trap. She watched as he stared the other man down. "You go ahead, Thompson. You've got the knife."

"Ah, but you've got the gun. You do have a gun, don't you? How fast do you think you are? Faster than this?" As though flaunting the fact that he had the upper hand, Virgil twirled the knife in the air, then caught it again. The movement was so fast a split second hadn't gone by. He laughed when Colin stepped forward slightly. "You like that, huh? Come on, try to catch it. I'll carve some new lines in your pretty face."

Julie couldn't wait any longer. Either way Colin was going to get hurt. Without a thought to her own safety, she ran the rest of the way to the button and slammed it down.

Then all hell did break loose. Seizing the opportunity Virgil lunged for Colin, knocking him back against the door. Thinking someone was going to leave, the dog tore off after both of them, knocking Julie off balance. The two men fell to the floor, grappling over the knife. They rolled around the plant, kicking over cans and recovery tanks. The dog growled and snapped, furious.

"Brutus!" Julie cried, running after him.

"Go," Colin told her. "Get out of here. Don't worry about the dog."

"Damn!" Virgil pushed at the animal, who snarled and snapped at his arm. "Get off, dog!"

Because he was on the floor, beneath the bigger man, Colin couldn't do anything except struggle as Virgil lay poised above him with the knife at his throat.

Julie didn't know what to do. She wasn't going to let Colin die. Not now. Not after all this. If Brutus could help so could she. She rushed forward, only to be shoved back against the wall. She heard her head crack as she fell against it with a loud thud. At least it gave Colin an opportunity to get away. Because Virgil had turned to her, Colin rolled across the floor out of range of the knife.

"Get out of here, Julie. Run!" he called as he sprang to his feet and faced off against Virgil again.

"Now you're dead, Marshall. No more games." Enraged, Virgil started after him, but the dog kept up his attack, biting the man's leg. Suddenly, angered beyond control, Virgil turned around, ready to sink the knife into the dog's back. But just then Brutus lunged for his throat, pushing him back against a cyanide vat.

The container was lined with lead, so the force of the fall didn't disturb the contents at all, but the hose dropped from the wall, spilling cyanide solution all over the floor. It ran across the tile creating a clear, wide splotch deceptively innocuous looking. Julie could only stare at the spot as the slight odor of almonds permeated the air. Within moments they'd all be dead.

Colin must have recognized the odor. "Run, Julie! Go!" Grabbing both her and the dog, he started to propel them from the room. They were closer to the office door than the outside door. To go out the back, they would have to cross the cyanide's path. All three of them started across the room. "What do we have to do to get out of here alive?" Colin asked her.

"Cover our faces as best as possible and try to hold our breaths till we reach the outside."

He mimicked the way she held her sleeve over her face. She found it hard to run without breathing. The fumes grew stronger with every passing second as the cyanide continued to spill out. They could hear Virgil coughing and staggering the other way. Since he was closer to the vat he had inhaled more fumes.

"Just a little bit longer," Colin said.

"He's going to die from poisoning! Colin, we've got to help him," she said as they threaded around the last vat.

"Julie, I'm not going to risk either of our lives for him. Don't worry about it. Hurry."

She felt like a murderer, but still she ran. Only she had underestimated her plant manager. They crashed through the front door and collapsed on the ground, gasping for air, just as he rounded the back, the knife still clutched in his hand. He started weaving across the parking lot, heading for his truck. Apparently he was still intent on getting away, even though he was gasping and coughing and wheezing.

"Oh, God." Julie knew the symptoms. Everyone who worked at Lustre, Inc. had been warned. The poison was replacing the oxygen in his blood stream, molecule by molecule. It would smother him slowly but surely, and he would die of suffocation. In the distance she could hear the fire department. The police pulled in, too. Several squad cars squealed to a halt beside Colin and her.

Virgil got most of the way across the parking lot. He grabbed onto the door handle of his truck, and for a moment it looked as if he had made it inside. Then he collapsed to the ground.

"Please, no." Julie closed her eyes and turned away.

"Don't look," Colin told her.

"It's so awful." It was ironic. If Colin's description of Norman Osgood's death had been accurate, Virgil had died in much the same way. By suffocation.

"Are you all right?" Colin asked after a long moment.

Not really certain, Julie took a shaky breath and glanced around at all the emergency personnel jumping out of squad cars and ambulances. They'd gotten there too late for Virgil. The fire department, however, arrived just in time to seal up the plant and clean up the spill. "Yes, I'm fine. What will happen now?"

"The police will talk to us."

"I guess we were lucky. We didn't get any fumes." They had been far enough away. "How's the dog?"

Brutus didn't look any the worse for wear. He was sitting beside them, waiting for someone to greet him. Colin patted his head. "Good boy. Good dog."

It took the fire department about half an hour to clean up the chemical spill. Though deadly, the spill was small and happened in an enclosed space. Colin spent the time talking to the Chicago police detective who had been in one of the squad cars that pulled up. When Colin came back, Julie had some questions of her own. "Virgil said you arrested him at one time."

Colin nodded. "I sent him up for manslaughter ten years ago. He actually killed the guy, but we couldn't prove it conclusively. He knew some things about another case the prosecutor wanted to convict, and pulled a plea bargain. He swore he'd get me."

"But why?"

He shrugged. "They all say that Julie. Looks like he got out of prison and went right back to his old habits. He probably worked with Osgood since he hit the streets. I'll bet if we look we'll find a paper trail for the past five years. When Osgood started to blackmail him, he decided to set me up for the murder and make good on his vow."

"What about the Cadillac? Virgil had his truck here the night Norman Osgood was killed. I saw him get into it. He left the plant right behind me."

"And somebody else was down the block in another car waiting to pick him up. I've got a feeling it was Virgil's wife, Amy. As you heard me tell Virgil, Amy Walker's the name on the Cadillac's registration."

"A woman his accomplice?" Julie asked, frowning.

"As we figured, two people had to be involved to do all those things," Colin said. "We mistakenly assumed it had to be two men, when all along it was Virgil and his wife, Amy."

Julie had a hard time believing it. Maybe women committed crimes of passion, but not crimes of violence. This had certainly been one of violence. "You think they planned to take the body all along?"

"No. The way I figure it, they killed Osgood somewhere else and brought him there."

"But why? That doesn't make sense."

"Sure it does. Osgood must have found out about Virgil's past and my involvement because Virgil aired his grudge on more than one occasion. Osgood then threatened to rat on Thompson if he didn't cooperate and give him a bigger cut. Instead Virgil killed him and set me up."

That explained why Virgil would kill his contact. "Why would he steal the body?"

"Because I took the gun and left before the police arrived. He had to figure out another way to pin the murder on me. Since it was a rainy night and they dumped Osgood on cement, there was no blood. No trace of anything."

"You think Virgil called the police?"

He shrugged. "Maybe. I'm sure if we check the dispatcher's log, like my friend Paul didn't, we'd get a gender. But that's irrelevant now. As I mentioned before, there were two calls to the station that night."

"But why would Virgil try to kill us later? Run us down?"

"I think he panicked. Maybe he figured we'd find something, and he'd better take care of things right then. Did he listen to your interview with the police?"

"Yes."

"You could have spooked him. After that he came to his senses and realized we had no way to identify him, or link him to the murder. His only recourse was to get us to surrender to police, and go on trial for the murder he committed."

"But what about my house, your apartment, the body in the refrigerator?"

He sighed. "We'll never know it all, Julie. My guess is that he was just hours ahead of us, sometimes minutes. He knew where we were going. In fact, we were followed, probably in Virgil's dark truck, which I wouldn't have spotted in the traffic. He must have trailed us from the plant last night, to the hotel, and he was the one who phoned the police about my whereabouts early this morning. He figured if he couldn't scare us into going to the police for protection, he could point the police to us." He flicked her a quick glance and nodded to the police detective he had spoken to earlier. "By the way, I had Paul run checks on Roger, and he conveyed this message. Your partner was in Chicago for exactly the reason you suggested—sausages and a case of his favorite beer."

Julie looked startled. "You're kidding?"

Colin laughed. "Nope. Apparently he couldn't find his favorite brands and decided to make the trip. You were right about your partners. They wouldn't get involved in such a mess."

Julie felt gladdened at that. At least she hadn't misjudged everyone around her, particularly the men she'd formed a business partnership with.

By then Detective Meier had appeared. After wandering over to glance at the plant manager, he came back to speak to Julie. "Looks like you found a body."

She nodded. "Only it's the wrong one," she said, referring to the body that had disappeared that Friday night.

"I hear you guys had a bit of an adventure this weekend," he said.

"You might say so," Julie agreed.

"Sorry. I didn't have anything to go on."

She knew he was apologizing for the other night. "Sure. I understand." When he whipped out his pen and paper she glanced at him. "I suppose you have to take a report."

"Yes, ma'am. The works," he said. "By the way, Marshall, the guy you decked is recuperating in the nursing station. He radioed a message on the way over. He said to tell you that you owe him three dinners."

Colin laughed and squeezed Julie's shoulder when she cast him a quizzical look. "I'll explain later."

The report took only a moment. They were almost done, when Brad pulled in, reporting for work. When they told him the story he was as stunned as everyone else. He stood staring at Virgil's car. Two ambulances threaded carefully through the crowded lot to it.

"Do you think we should call Roger?" Brad asked.

"Yes, as soon as things calm down here," Julie answered.

"What about Virgil's wife?"

"She's already at the police station," the detective piped in. "I understand he threatened to kill her if she didn't cooperate."

Julie shook her head, not understanding. "How could he have been so sick and we didn't know it?"

"Humanity. You're one of the nicer people in this world, Julie."

She sighed. It was as good an explanation as any. "I suppose."

"Do you need me for anything?" Brad went on. "I thought I'd better oversee the plant emergency and make sure employees leave today."

"I'm fine. You go on." Julie said. She was just so sad. "See you tomorrow?"

Her partner paused. "Sure you don't want to take a vacation?"

"Maybe. I'll think about it."

"Just let me know. Okay?" He turned to Colin and held out his hand in greeting. "Nice meeting you. Take good care of her."

"Right," Colin answered. "I will."

Julie sat down on the ground next to Brutus, watching her partner leave. As if sensing her despondency, the dog whined and nudged her. When she placed her arm around his neck and hugged him, Colin shook his head and laughed. "I spent months training him to hold people at bay. The leash just shoots the ploy to pieces. You ready to go?"

"Where?" What would they do now? It was over. Odd, everything felt so anticlimactic again.

"I thought we'd check into that spaceship to Mars."

"What?" She frowned at him. Sometimes he talked nonsense. Then she remembered their conversation that first night about solving the murder.

"Either that, or we need to make arrangements to visit Jordan," he went on.

Julie was still puzzled. "Why Jordan?"

"Isn't that where the Dead Sea is located? I figure the way you reacted to that railing last night, we'd be better off there than the Himalayas."

"We?"

"You and me." Funny, his face had turned ruddy, as though he were unsure of himself, and he raked a hand through his bronze hair. "As on a honeymoon? Julie, do you believe in love in forty-eight hours?"

"What are you talking about, Colin?"

"I love you, Red, even though it's only been three days."

"Oh, Colin." She felt so touched.

"Brutus and I agree we'd be willing to give up our bachelorhood if you'd come live with us." He shrugged. "If you want, I'll even give you a week or two to get to know me."

Julie didn't need a week. She didn't need another moment. It wouldn't matter if she'd known him for two days or two weeks or two centuries. She loved him, and she would love him forever. She stood up and brushed off her jeans. "How will I get out of the apartment?"

"That's a problem. Once I get you, I intend to keep you. Just as any good host would, right?"

She pretended to consider his offer. "Tell me, Mr. Manners, what kind of china do you like?"

"Anything old."

"I like blue patterned china."

He laughed. "I'll bet you liked Officer Friendly when you were a kid."

"What does that have to do with the subject?"

"Nothing. I just wish you'd hurry and give me your answer. I'm beginning to feel we should go for a car ride or something."

She shook her head emphatically. "No car rides. And actually, I'd like to skip the Dead Sea. Think you could afford a suite at the Bradford for the night, instead?"

His smile dazzled her. "I think that can be arranged."

"The one with the whirlpool tub? We never did get around to using it."

"As I recall, we were rudely interrupted."

She took his hand. "Then come on. I think you'd better meet my folks."

Colin frowned. "Why your folks?"

"Because my mother trusts me," Julie said.

"I see."

"You know, sometime we have to take a trip to Georgia," she went on as they walked across the parking lot to his car. "I want to see the farm."

"It's just onions."

"And your heritage." That was awfully important. She wanted to know everything about him, what he'd been like as a kid, that scar on his cheek, the way he thought, the things he enjoyed, the way he walked, talked, lived, loved.

They were almost to his car, when she spotted his sister's station wagon. "Should we return it to her?"

"We can call." He opened the door. Brutus climbed in the back. "By the way, how'd you get him out of the house?" Colin asked.

"I told you, I tricked him."

He glanced at her with admiration in his eyes. "There's one thing I like about you, Julie Hunter. You're very resourceful."

She smiled secretively. "Just wait until you see the plans I have for the bubble bath."

He laughed and got in his side. "Which way, lady?"

Lynda Ward's TOUCH THE STARS

...the final book in the *The Welles Family Trilogy*

Lynda Ward's TOUCH THE STARS... the final book in the Welles Family Trilogy. All her life Kate Welles Brock has sought to win the approval of her wealthy and powerful father, even going as far as to marry Burton Welles's handpicked successor to the Corminco Corporation.

Now, with her marriage in tatters behind her, Kate is getting the first taste of what it feels like to really live. Her glorious romance with the elusive Paul Florian is opening up a whole new world to her.... Kate is as determined to win the love of her man as she is to prove to her father that she is the logical choice to succeed him as head of Corminco....

Don't miss TOUCH THE STARS, a Harlequin Superromance coming to you in September.

If you missed the first two books of this exciting trilogy, #317 RACE THE SUN and #321 LEAP THE MOON, and would like to order them, send your name, address and zip or postal code, along with a check or money order for $2.95 for each book ordered (plus $1.00 postage and handling) payable to Harlequin Reader Service to:

In the U.S.	In Canada
901 Fuhrmann Blvd.	P.O. Box 609
Box 1396	Ft. Erie, Ontario
Buffalo, NY 14240-9954	L2A 5X3

LYNDA-1C

ATTRACTIVE, SPACE SAVING BOOK RACK

Display your most prized novels on this handsome and sturdy book rack. The hand-rubbed walnut finish will blend into your library decor with quiet elegance, providing a practical organizer for your favorite hard-or soft-covered books.

Only $9.95

Approximately 16" x 8" when assembled

Assembles in seconds!

To order, rush your name, address and zip code, along with a check or money order for $10.70* ($9.95 plus 75¢ postage and handling) payable to *Harlequin Reader Service*:

> Harlequin Reader Service
> Book Rack Offer
> 901 Fuhrmann Blvd.
> P.O. Box 1396
> Buffalo, NY 14269-1396
>
> *Offer not available in Canada.*

*New York and Iowa residents add appropriate sales tax.

ABANDON YOURSELF TO

Temptation ™

In September's Harlequin Temptation books you'll get more than just terrific sexy romance—you'll get $2 worth of **Jovan Musk** fragrance coupons **plus** an opportunity to get a very special, unique nightshirt.

Harlequin's most sensual series will also be featuring four of Temptation's favourite authors writing the Montclair Emeralds quartet.

Harlequin Temptation in September—too hot to miss!

JOVAN-1